THEIR ROYAL
BABY GIFT

THEIR ROYAL BABY GIFT

KANDY SHEPHERD

MILLS & BOON

First published in Great Britain 2020
by Mills & Boon, an imprint of HarperCollins*Publishers*
1 London Bridge Street, London, SE1 9GF
www.harpercollins.co.uk
HarperCollins *Publishers*
1st Floor, Watermarque Building, Ringsend Road
Dublin 4, Ireland
Large Print edition 2021
© 2020 Harlequin Books S.A.

Special thanks and acknowledgement are given to Kandy Shepherd for her contribution to the Christmas at the Harrington Park Hotel collection.

ISBN: 978-0-263-28989-3

MIX
Paper from
responsible sources
FSC
www.fsc.org FSC® C007454

Printed and bound in Great Britain
by CPI Group (UK) Ltd, Croydon, CR0 4YY

To Deanna Lang, with many thanks.
Not just for your ongoing friendship
but for your help in creating my hero
Edward's character and background.

CHAPTER ONE

SALLY HARRINGTON WAS having fun pretending to be an awestruck tourist as she gawked at the rooftop garden with its towering palm trees, lush tropical plants and enormous infinity swimming pool, all poised a breathtaking sixty storeys high above the city of Singapore. The resort in the sky exceeded all her expectations—it was nothing short of spectacular. No wonder a well-heeled international crowd made it their playground. She snapped photo after photo on her phone's camera, even taking a few selfies in pursuit of authenticity.

She was playing Sally the tourist because she wanted to keep her real interest in the roof garden secret. Truth was, she was in Singapore on a confidential research mission on behalf of the iconic Harrington Park Hotel in London that had recently come back into her family's hands.

She wasn't here as a holidaymaker but as a professional designer. Some might say she was conducting a little industrial espionage—whatever you called it, she didn't want to be caught out. The aesthetics of the roof garden interested her, but also the logistics of how it had been created. Structural support for the weight of the pool and the plantings? Materials brought in by helicopter or crane? Details were vital—she only had seven weeks to create a fabulous roof garden of her own for the splashy, invitation-only Christmas Eve relaunch of the Harrington Park.

'Hotel royalty' *Celebrity* magazine called the Harringtons. It was impossible for Sally and her two brothers to fly under the radar in London but here, so far from home, it was easier to be anonymous as she sought inspiration for her ambitious project. And, she had to admit, she'd jumped at the chance to take a break from the total upheaval of the ordered life she had fought so hard to achieve.

First had been the decision by her and her twin brother James—Jay to family and friends—to use a substantial inheritance from their grandmother to bid for the Harrington Park when it suddenly came onto the market. The luxury hotel on Regent's Park had been in their family for more than one hundred years until their unscrupulous stepfather had taken it over and run it down. She and Jay had been thwarted in their purchase by a mystery buyer who had turned out to be their estranged older brother, Hugo. Sally hadn't seen Hugo for seventeen years since he'd left their family when she'd been ten years old and he seventeen. Now he expected her to forgive all and work with him to restore both the hotel and their family's pride.

Jay, a top chef with his own award-winning restaurant, had found it easier than she to fall in with Hugo's plans to bring the hotel back to its former glory. Sally had agreed to oversee the refurbishment of the interiors because she couldn't bear to see how shabby they had become. She'd said yes to the urban roof garden too, in spite of her initial protests that there simply wasn't time to undertake such an ambitious project.

But that didn't mean she'd thawed towards Hugo. She still remembered her distress when she'd woken up on Christmas morning all those years ago to find her beloved older brother had run away without so much as a goodbye. On top of her father's death and her mother's marriage to a man Sally had despised and distrusted, Hugo's betrayal had been too much to forgive. And now he was back and flinging olive branches at her. A break away in tropical Singapore from both her older brother and chilly London had seemed like a very good idea indeed.

With the pool behind her, Sally edged back to get a final shot that would encompass the plantings of glorious pink and purple orchids around the restaurant. The tropical afternoon sun beat down on her arms, bare in her sleeveless white linen dress. She thought vaguely about applying more sun cream. Then, distracted, she tripped. In a split second of panicked disbelief and horror she realised she was about to topple backwards, arms windmilling, into the swimming pool.

She was aware of a collective gasp from the onlookers around the other side of the pool. Then she lost control of her balance and fell, hitting the water on her back. She tried to scream but all she managed was a splutter as the cold water engulfed her and she went under. Her long hair floated over her face, her wedge-heeled sandals made it difficult to kick, her dress tangled around her legs and dragged her down as she struggled. She choked on her terror.

She couldn't swim.

* * *

Edward Chen was striding past the pool, intent on the agenda of his next meeting for the afternoon, when he saw the woman with the long chestnut hair fall in the water with a splash. Heard the gasps and laughter from the people seated around the other side of the pool. Like him, they no doubt expected her to surface straight away and swim to the edge. But she didn't. The woman momentarily broke the surface of the water, panic and terror etched on her face, then went under again, leaving only a few bubbles floating on the surface.

With no thought to his Italian tailor-made linen suit or his handmade leather shoes, Edward dived in. Just a few strong strokes and he was with her. He grabbed her under her arms and kicked hard to take them both to the surface.

Once clear, he trod water to keep them both afloat. The woman blinked the water from her eyes, coughed and spluttered, took in deep gulps of air, gripped his shoulders hard. She tried to say something, but the words were lost in another fit of coughing. Edward realised she was trying to thank him.

'Don't say anything—just catch your breath,' he said.

He steered her towards the shallow steps that led out of the pool. As she shakily emerged from the water, still clinging tightly to him, there was muted applause from the people who had only minutes before laughed at the sight of a fully dressed woman toppling into the pool. Edward cursed under his breath in his own language. Anyone with a cell phone was a potential paparazzo.

Did they know who he was?

The woman's eyes widened in alarm. 'Please,' she managed to choke out, 'get me away from here. I… I…don't want to draw attention to myself.'

Edward had every reason not to want to draw attention to himself either. Especially in the company of an attractive young Englishwoman. Even drenched and dripping she was lovely: heart-shaped face, grey eyes, tall and slender. Under the water, with her dark chestnut hair waving around her, she'd looked like a mermaid.

She was shivering, whether chilled from the cold water of the pool or from shock he couldn't be sure. Edward was wet through himself and his shoes squelched with each step.

He couldn't be seen like this.

He came from a family that had been rocked to its foundations by scandal. It was vital for his family's future that he stayed free of it. He dreaded the innuendo and speculation the media would build around his good deed if they got wind of it. The woman's wet dress clung to her body, making no secret of her curves. She was a scandal in the making.

He grabbed a striped towel from a stack on a nearby lounger and threw it around her shoulders, another one around himself. 'Keep your head down and walk as quickly as you can,' he said.

She attempted a faster pace but stumbled and he had to put his arm around her to keep her upright. He scarcely broke his stride to pick up the phone she'd dropped when she'd fallen.

'Are you hurt?'

'Only…only my pride.'

'Are you staying at this hotel?'

She shook her head and wet strands flew around her face, sending droplets of water onto him. 'I… I only came here for lunch. My hotel is in the older part of town.'

'I'm in the penthouse here. There's a private elevator down to my suite. I'll take you there.'

'Please.' She was still shivering, and her eyes didn't look quite focused.

He had to get her—and himself—out of here. Edward kept his arm around Ms Mermaid as he ushered her to the discreet private elevator. If people didn't recognise him, a scandal could be averted.

Within minutes they were in the expansive suite where he was living while his Singapore house was being gutted and refurbished. He slammed the door behind them and slumped in relief. No one with a camera could follow him here. He turned back into the room. Then realised he had swapped one problem for another. Standing opposite him, dripping water on the marble floor of his hotel suite, was a beautiful stranger—and her presence here could so easily be misconstrued.

'Thank you,' she said. 'I could have drowned.' Her eyes were huge, her lush mouth trembled. Hair wet and dripping, make-up smudged around her eyes, she was breathtakingly lovely. A red-blooded male, no matter how chivalrous, could not fail to feel a stirring of attraction. 'I… I can't swim, not enough to save myself. But you…you saved me.'

'It was the right thing to do,' Edward said gruffly. He had been brought up to follow a strict code of duty and honour. To help a person in danger was second nature. And there'd been something so desperate in her expression when she'd gone under for the second time. He could not have denied her silent cry for help.

'You were a gentleman. No one else came to my rescue. I've never been so frightened in my life. I really thought… I thought it was the end.'

She started to shake and shiver, her teeth chattering. Edward thought back to his first aid training. His family's country compound back home was on a private beach. There he'd learned to swim and to keep both himself and others safe in the water. She didn't appear injured. She didn't need CPR. What this woman needed was warmth and comfort. He hesitated for only a second before he pulled her into his arms. And was shocked by how good she felt there, her curves pressed to him, how instantly his body reacted to her.

* * *

Sally's thoughts raced. She must be in shock. Why else would she unquestioningly follow an unknown man to his hotel room? Why would she press her body so close to a total stranger? And welcome his comforting hug? His warmth and strength seemed to infuse her, calm her, bring her breathing back to normal. Her reaction could only be from shock. Or some kind of insanity. How else could she explain how much she was enjoying his embrace, the feel of his hard chest, his strong arms around her?

She'd been too long without the intimate touch of a man.

'I can't thank you enough.' Her voice was muffled against his shoulder.

'There's no need to thank me again,' he said. His deep, resonant voice with a blur of an American accent to his impeccable English, sent shivers up her spine. Luckily, she'd only just stopped shivering from shock so hoped he wouldn't notice.

This was crazy.

There was something deeply disconcerting about how readily she had relaxed into the embrace of a stranger in that unguarded moment between panic and the relief of rescue. She pulled away from her rescuer, stuttered her thanks. Without his warmth it was chilly in the air-conditioned room. She wrapped her arms around herself, but it was no consolation for the loss of his hug.

Under the water, Sally's only thought had been how grateful she was for the man's help. As he'd guided her out of the pool she'd realised he was very strong and very competent. Now she looked—really looked—up at him. At five foot ten she was tall, but her rescuer was so much taller. Just as she was getting her voice back, she lost it again. The man was catch-your-breath handsome. So good-looking all she could do was stare. Young—older perhaps than her twenty-seven, but not by much—black hair, slashed cheekbones, *hot*. Although his clothes were dripping all over the floor, his linen suit was obviously well cut and stylish, his watch worth a small fortune. She hoped it was waterproof.

'I... I...tripped,' she stuttered.

'I saw,' he said seriously, so seriously she suspected he was trying not to smile.

'The strap on my sandal, it...er...it's a bit loose.' Why did she feel she had to explain? she thought, cross at herself for losing her cool. Her heart pounded, not with residual panic but with awareness of how close she stood to this gorgeous, gorgeous man.

'You don't need to explain,' he said. 'It was obviously an accident.'

'It was so sudden. I… I…' In contrast to the intense heat and humidity outside, the air-conditioning in his suite was icy and she was very wet. She sneezed. 'Sorry.' She sneezed again.

'We need to get you out of those wet clothes,' her rescuer said.

Sally stilled. Fought a crazy, unbidden thrill at his words which she again blamed on shock. She backed towards the door. 'I don't think so,' she said.

He frowned. 'I didn't mean *that*. I need to get out of mine too.'

What had she got herself into? She gauged the distance between herself, him and the door.

Her rescuer slammed his hand against his forehead. 'That's not at all what I meant.'

'What do you mean? Because I'm thinking I need to get the heck out of here.'

He shrugged. 'You're welcome to do that. It would be easier for me. But you did say you didn't want to draw attention to yourself. Traipsing out of the hotel and hailing a cab with your clothes dripping wet might just—'

'I get it,' she said.

She needed to stay incognito. The media had long tentacles.

Harrington heiress seen escaping hotel in Singapore!

The speculation would blow her cover. The drama surrounding the return of Hugo had focused new attention on the 'photogenic Harrington twins' and their older brother. There were other spectacular roof gardens she wanted to inspect while she was in Singapore—the city was famous for them. That was her mission. The reopening of the Harrington Park was a big deal. She didn't want to be the one to take the surprise out of the relaunch. As well, deep down, she had to admit she wanted to impress Hugo with her talent and skill. Drawing unwelcome media attention was not the way to go.

'There are four bathrooms in this suite,' her rescuer said. 'I suggest you take the nearest one and I'll take the furthest one. You can lock the door. We can reconvene in the living room when you're done.'

'I'm not sure…' This whole scenario seemed somehow too intimate, too laced with the threat of danger.

'You don't know me, but I assure you that you can trust me,' he said. She saw only sincerity in his narrowed eyes. He was powerfully masculine but there was nothing threatening in his stance. His tone was commanding without being over-bearing, which would have sent her running a mile, wet clothes or not.

Sally was not a person to act on impulse. She liked to plan, consider, have everything in its place before she made a decision. Yet somehow she felt she could trust the man who had saved her from the pool. Her late mother's words came back to her: *'Darling, most people are basically good and would help you rather than hurt you.'* Of course that hadn't applied to her stepfather.

'Okay,' she said, surprising herself at her will-ingness to take such a risk.

Her rescuer showed Sally to a bathroom, being careful, she noticed, to maintain a respectful dis-tance from her. He didn't linger but turned on his heel and strode away. He appeared sophisticated, urbane, but the effect was somewhat ruined by the rather rude squelching noises his waterlogged shoes made on the marble floor. Sally unsuccessfully tried to smother a laugh.

He turned around to face her and he shrugged self-deprecatingly. 'I know,' he said with a half-smile.

'The leather will be ruined,' she said.

'I have other shoes,' he said.

He set off again and she swore he stepped harder to exaggerate the noise made by his wet shoes. She laughed, this time making no effort to conceal it. He laughed too as he left a trail of wet footsteps behind him, then taking his shoes off before he entered what she assumed must be the living area.

With a smile still on her face, Sally slipped into the bathroom. Locked the door. Noted—just in case—there was a phone on the wall. Handsome and charming he might be, but her rescuer was still a total stranger.

Her cell phone had suffered a cracked screen from its drop to the tiled surrounds of the pool but seemed otherwise intact. To keep it from further damage, she tucked it into the tiny travel shoulder bag she had worn slung across her body. Thankfully the bag had lived up to its claim of being impenetrable.

As she stripped off her wet clothes, she couldn't help but admire the bathroom with a professional eye, noting the top-grade marble, the expensive fittings, the unstinting luxury. She wanted a more traditional, very English look for the Harrington Park but there was a lesson to be learned from this hotel's devotion to guest comfort.

Could she ever allow herself to switch off from work?

The Ice Queen, she knew people called her. Nicknamed for both her ruthless devotion to her business and her reputation for never letting relationships get deeper than dating. The name hurt, but she never let anyone see that. It wasn't that she wanted to be on her own. She needed love and intimacy as much as anyone else. But she always seemed to go for men who were unattainable.

Her first major crush at boarding school had been on a darkly handsome Spanish boy—until he'd told her he wanted to be a priest and needed to remain celibate. She had shared her first kisses with another schoolmate—then he'd confessed he was experimenting but was pretty sure he was gay. They'd become good friends instead of lovers, although it had taken a long time for her not to be half in love with him. Her most recent Mr Out-of-Reach had been a quite well-known actor, recently divorced and determined to avoid commitment—he'd made that very clear when she'd met him. His ruthless dumping of her had been more than a year ago. The press coverage had not been kind. She'd been too wounded to bother with dating since. Work had become her refuge from romance.

She showered and shampooed her hair with the expensive toiletries supplied, revelling in being warm and safe. Then towelled herself dry in a decadently fluffy towel—they must have only this quality of towel for the Harrington Park. She dried her hair into its usual sleek lines, taking particular care with the styling. Call it vanity, or something more deeply instinctive, but she had an urge to look better than the drowned rat her handsome rescuer had pulled out of the pool. She couldn't do much for the smeared make-up but tidy it up with a tissue.

No way could she get back into her sodden clothes that she had thrown into the bathtub. In fact, she didn't ever want to wear that dress again. She shuddered at the memory of how the midi-length skirt had tangled itself around her legs, hindering her attempts to swim. Her sandals appeared to be a lost cause. Still, she did her best to squeeze the water out of her dress and underwear. Perhaps there was a tumble dryer somewhere in this suite, but she doubted it. People who could afford to stay in luxury penthouses didn't do their own laundry.

Unless she intended to stay in the bathroom until her clothes dripped dry, she had no choice but to slip, naked, into the hotel's thick, velvety black bathrobe. She wrapped it right around her waist for total coverage and belted it tightly. Feeling somewhat revived, she opened the door and padded barefoot on the marble floor towards the living room of the suite.

CHAPTER TWO

THE ENORMOUS LIVING room of her rescuer's suite opened to a balcony with a view to the Gardens by the Bay and out to Marina Bay and the ships waiting in the harbour. The amazing futuristic tree-like structures of the Supertree Grove and the adjacent Flower Dome and Cloud Forest conservatories were on her to-do list for the next day.

Her Sir Galahad was fixing drinks at the full-sized bar. He was dressed casually in wheat-coloured linen trousers and a white silk knit T-shirt. Sally could not help but appreciate his back view, broad shoulders tapering to a very appealing butt.

At her entry to the room, he turned. She had to swallow hard at how good he looked. Dry, his hair was spiky and black, and the T-shirt showed sculpted muscles, smooth brown skin. For a long moment their gazes met. A current of curiosity and speculation seemed to crackle between them.

He was seriously hot.

She was the first to drop her eyes.

'I could do with a drink—how about you?' he said. He smiled. Sally didn't think he could get any better-looking, but the smile did it—perfect white teeth and eyes that smiled too.

All caution about accepting drinks from a stranger fled her mind. She had nearly drowned; a drink was very much in order. 'A Singapore Sling?'

He smiled again. 'I'm no barman. But I can order one from room service.'

The hotel where she was staying was home to the iconic cocktail. She'd try one later. 'Dry white wine then, please,' she said.

When he handed her the wine, she noticed the absence of a wedding band. He was very careful to avoid any accidental touching of fingers, but even so they brushed. Just that slightest of touches sent a shiver of awareness through her.

Did he notice?

He was drinking black label whisky, no ice. She took a sip from her wine and willed herself to relax.

'Your wet clothes,' he said.

'The hotel laundry. I thought…'

'Do you have time to wait for that?'

Sally had lost all track of time. She glanced at her watch—thankfully waterproof. It was already past five p.m. 'No,' she said. But would she be happy travelling back to her hotel in a bathrobe? Perhaps she had no choice.

He cleared his throat. 'I've taken the liberty of ordering you a new dress from one of the hotel boutiques.'

'You *what*?' Oddly, she didn't call him out on his high-handed action—which it most certainly was—but rather blurted, 'How did you know my size?' He was exceedingly handsome, obviously wealthy; perhaps he often bought clothes for women.

'My sister is about your size, although she isn't as tall. She often shops there on her visits to Singapore. I asked the manager to find something that would fit her. They'll send it up to the room soon.'

'My wallet survived its plunge in the pool. My credit cards should be okay. I'll call down—'

'No need. It's already paid for.'

'But I can't possibly accept that. I must repay you.'

He made a dismissive gesture that had a certain arrogance. 'Too difficult. I don't take credit cards. It's nothing. Please accept the dress as a souvenir of your visit to Singapore.'

Sally was too flabbergasted for coherent speech. 'But I… No.' It was out of the question to accept such a gift from a stranger. She knew his room number. The boutique's details would no doubt be on their shopping bag. She would phone through a payment from her and a refund for him after she got back to her hotel.

'I've also ordered some food from room service,' he said.

'But I… I'm not hungry.'

'You can take the meal or leave it. However, you've had quite a shock. You might find you need some food.' The door buzzer sounded. 'That's either room service or your dress.'

An obsequious waiter wheeled in a trolley and placed silver trays on the glass-topped dining table. Delicious smells of spicy food wafted upwards and Sally's appetite suddenly revived. But it was a stretch from being rescued by a stranger to sharing a meal with him.

A meal made it feel more like a date.

The waiter lifted the silver domes from the trays to reveal a *dim sum* feast—small plates and bamboo steamers of bite-sized snacks. Some Sally recognised, others she did not.

'A taste of Singapore,' said her rescuer—or was he now her host? 'Like the city itself, the flavours are Chinese, Malaysian, Indian and Western.'

The waiter briefly described each of the dishes. They included fluffy steamed savoury buns, dumplings full of spicy broth, pan-fried oysters, tiny western-style sliders, vegetables she didn't recognise as well as the more familiar spring rolls and samosas. The waiter was deferential in the extreme; he couldn't have used the term 'sir' more often and he bowed deeply before he left the room. Her host must be a generous tipper.

Sally looked longingly at the *dim sum*. 'I… I'm not sure it's appropriate to…to linger here.'

But she was still in the hotel bathrobe, her clothes too wet to wear. She was trapped… although she didn't feel in danger. Call it instinct or hunch but she didn't think her rescuer meant her harm. Quite the opposite—she had felt so safe and comforted in his arms. Safe and something so much more—a stirring of a long subdued sensual interest, an undefined longing for something that had always remained out of her reach.

'If you don't want to eat, I'll have the food taken away.' He motioned to call the waiter back.

'Yes. I mean *no*. Don't have it taken away. It looks too good to resist.'

He smiled that very appealing smile. 'You've had a big shock. The food at this hotel is good. You might find a snack is just what you need.'

'Thank you. I… I appreciate your thoughtfulness.' The *dim sum* was making her mouth water.

He waved away her thanks. 'It's nothing.'

It was actually extraordinarily generous and hospitable of him. A different kind of man might have pulled her from the pool and sent her on her way. Or ignored her plight and left her to flounder.

'Where do I start?' Sally said, once she was seated at one of the dining chairs opposite her host.

Just like on a date.

'Wherever you like.' He poured her hot Chinese tea in a small porcelain cup without handles. Sally took the cup with thanks and sipped, looking over its edge at him. It was a long time since she had been in the company of a man as strikingly attractive as this one.

She was dressed in a bathrobe and sharing a

meal with a handsome stranger. All in all, it was a slightly bizarre situation she found herself in. Bizarre but, in its own way, exciting.

She tried to keep her eyes on the food but was unable to stop herself from darting glances at him. Every time she found something new. A sexy cleft in his chin. A full, sensuous mouth. Smooth skin she wanted to reach out and touch.

'Can you use chopsticks?' he asked.

'Not very skilfully, but yes.' She deftly picked up a prawn roll and transferred it to her bowl.

'I see you need no tuition at all,' he said, amused.

'I have a favourite Chinese restaurant in London,' she said. 'So I get some practice.'

He put down his own chopsticks on a silver rest. 'You're from London. Are you on vacation in Singapore?'

She nodded. A working holiday—but he didn't need to know that.

'Is it your first visit?'

'Yes,' she said. 'I only arrived here this morning.'

Several of the wealthy foreign clients of her high-end interior design business had been so pleased with her work on their residences in the

UK, they had invited her to work for them in their home countries. She flew frequently to Dubai and Mumbai in particular. But never before to Singapore.

'There's a lot to see in Singapore,' her rescuer said.

She'd like to see more of him.

His comment seemed somewhat trite—but what else did she expect from a conversation with a stranger? Especially a stranger she had met in such an extraordinary circumstance. As far as she could tell on such brief acquaintance, they had no common ground. But wasn't that the point of such conversations—to establish common ground?

This is not a date, she had to remind herself again.

She answered in kind. 'I'm only here for a few days and I'm determined to see as much as I can.'

He paused. 'Just before you fell in the pool I noticed you taking photographs of the rooftop garden.'

Sally's heart stopped. Was the game up? Had he picked her for an industrial spy? Did he have a connection to the hotel? She rushed a reply.

'It's impressive, isn't it? Especially those towering palm trees and the exquisite orchids. I... I probably took way too many snaps. Gardening is somewhat of a hobby.'

'Really?'

His obvious scepticism was no surprise. No one else in her social set shared her interest in gardening. That was a pastime for parents, grandparents even. But she had been deeply unhappy at her prestigious boarding school and the garden had become her refuge. The head gardener had taken her under her wing and Sally's interest had developed from there. After she'd left school, she had even started an apprenticeship in garden design until she'd realised interior design was her overwhelming passion. Since she'd had her own business, she'd been able to combine both her interests.

'I'm fascinated by the challenges of planting such a large garden on a rooftop,' she said.

'There are many such gardens in Singapore.'

'So I believe. This morning I saw a flourishing garden on top of a bus. I couldn't believe it. You should have seen how many photos I took of that.'

He smiled. 'I haven't seen such a bus myself. I'll take your word for it.'

She indicated with a wave the view of Supertree Grove below. 'I'm heading down there tomorrow; those gardens look amazing.'

Was that too much information? Did he believe her? Did it matter if he did or he didn't?

For a long moment their eyes again met in a gaze too long and too intent for strangers. Her spine tingled with awareness of just how attractive she found him. Was that an answering interest in his dark eyes? How would she know? She was notorious for misreading men. And when it came to flirting, the Ice Queen didn't have a clue.

She tore her gaze away, reached with her chopsticks for an oyster. Her hand wasn't steady and she missed the first time, the chopsticks clicking against each other. *Flirting.* No way should she even be entertaining that thought. But where was the harm in finding out a little more about him?

Her words came out in a rush. 'You're visiting Singapore too? I mean, you're staying in a hotel, so I assume—'

'I'm here on business. I fly out tomorrow.'

There was no reason she should feel so disappointed.

'What line of business?'

'Telecommunications. And you?'

'Interior design.'

'Commercial or residential?'

'Mainly residential,' she said.

The exception being the urgent refurbishment of an iconic hotel that bore her family name.

'In Singapore?'

Was that a trick question?

'Not right now. I'm enjoying being a tourist. Exploring. Seeing the gardens. As I…er…said.' She was annoyed at herself for the nervous edge to her voice. She prided herself on being in control, not letting anything get to her. Let alone a man.

'You did,' he said. He certainly wasn't a person to rush into mindless conversation. Her rescuer had a calm way of speaking that might have, in different circumstances, evoked more of a sensible response from her. But she found him so darn desirable she found it difficult to concentrate on anything else but imagining what it might be like to kiss him.

She picked up a dumpling with her chopsticks and popped it into her mouth, savoured it, gave a sigh of appreciation. 'Delicious—everything is delicious.' She put down her chopsticks, looked up at him. 'You were right about me needing food.'

'I'm glad you're feeling better.' He sounded genuinely pleased he had met her needs. It wasn't something she was used to. The men in her world were not the kind, caring type—with the exception of her brother Jay. This man was considerate, caring and hot. It was a dizzying combination.

She needed to make her gratitude clear. 'Thank you. For rescuing me. For making me feel less embarrassed about making such a fool of myself. For all of this.' With the wave of her chopsticks, she encompassed the meal, the room. 'You've been such a gentleman.'

Hidden beneath her polite words was an urgent subtext she would never allow to be voiced. What she'd appreciated the most was the pleasure of being held in his arms. The intimacy of his hug. Even the memory of it sent arousal tingling through her body.

She wanted more.

Edward gritted his teeth. If only Ms Mermaid knew just how very ungentlemanly he was feeling. His unexpected guest made a hotel dressing

gown look like the sexiest of evening gowns—
and he'd become obsessed with the desire to slide
it off her.

His heart had started to pound as she'd made
her way from the bathroom to the living room.
The black velvet had swished around her legs,
highlighting the alluring sway of her hips, giving him enticing glimpses of slender pale legs.
He strongly suspected she was naked under the
gown. The hotel tried to anticipate a guest's
every need, but underwear for a woman whose
clothes had suffered a plunge in the swimming
pool was almost certainly not stocked in the
bathroom.

Now, as she sat opposite him, the lapels of the
dressing gown had fallen open just enough to
reveal a tantalising hint of cleavage. Her hair
swung sleek over her shoulders, reddish glints
caught by the late afternoon sunlight filtering
through the glass doors that led to the balcony.
She was beautiful.
His heart pounded harder just looking at her.
More than just beautiful.
He wasn't a man prey to instant infatuation.
Such madness was not to be tolerated in the life
that had been mapped out for him. Yet he was

utterly fascinated by this woman who he had, on an uncharacteristic impulse, pulled to safety from the pool.

The intense attraction wasn't just about her good looks. It wasn't just sexual—although that was certainly there. *Man, was it there.* There was something about the light in her eyes, her generous smile, the musical tone of her voice. It was an indefinable pull towards this woman that was impossible to explain or analyse because he had never before felt anything like it.

He wanted to lean across the table, take her hand in his, make an amusing comment about what an unusual way it was to meet. Tell her he was glad that he had happened to be walking by as she tripped. Confess he was a great believer in fate and that fate had brought her to him. Ask her if she was married, engaged, promised—she wore no rings on either hand. Suggest that the *dim sum* could be followed by dinner in the private dining room of the most fashionable club in Singapore.

But the reality of Edward's situation punched into him to deflate every such fantasy. He could take none of those actions. He was thirty-one years old and under pressure from his father to make a politically advantageous marriage. An arranged marriage, with a bride chosen for him by his parents, the King and Queen. As Crown Prince of the south-east Asian kingdom of Tianlipin, Edward was duty-bound to do what was best not for him but for his country.

His father's dissolute older twin brothers had brought disgrace to the kingdom. The corrupt former King—older than his identical twin by ten minutes—had died in dubious circumstances. His twin and heir had been arrested for embezzlement on a grand scale, forced to relinquish his claim to the throne and live in exile. Edward's father—the youngest brother—had had to step up to the throne, clear up the mess his brothers had made and regain the trust of their people.

The current King's rule was a very different one, based on a strong moral code, honour, service and above all duty. That had been drummed into Edward ever since his father had ascended the throne when Edward had been ten years old. He'd gone from carefree son of a third son to Crown Prince. That was when the choice of how he, as heir to the throne, might live his life had been taken away from him.

Edward's future wife had been chosen for him,

although they were not as yet engaged. She was ten years younger than him. There had been one awkward meeting between them. Sparks had not flown. Certainly not on his side and not, Edward suspected, on her side either. In fact, he wasn't sure he'd even liked the young Princess.

But his rogue uncles had not only put a dent in his country's treasury with their decadent excesses but also soured relations with neighbouring kingdoms with which Tianlipin had formed alliances centuries ago. Marriage to the Princess, daughter of their closest ally and trading partner would, according to Edward's parents, go a long way to righting the lingering wrongs of his uncles. Bound by duty and honour, he had had little choice but to agree.

Edward had had girlfriends. There had been a certain amount of freedom when he had studied for post-graduate degrees in England and America as plain Edward Chen instead of Chen Wangzi—wangzi meaning prince in his language—Prince Chen of Tianlipin. To English speakers he was Prince Edward. However, because he was unlikely to be able to choose his own bride, he had always held back on his emotions. Only once had he allowed himself to fall in love, with disastrous consequences for both himself and his 'unsuitable' girlfriend.

But now he was about to become engaged, girlfriends were off the table. He would never be allowed to follow his heart. Or ask a beautiful stranger he had rescued from a swimming pool on a date.

He realised he had not acknowledged her thanks, had probably been looking at her for longer than politeness dictated. 'I'm happy I was able to help you,' he said stiffly.

Conversation had flowed easily but now it appeared she was as lost for words as he was. He found himself unable to tear his gaze from her and she flushed high on her cheekbones. But she didn't drop her eyes. If he was mesmerised so, it seemed, was she.

The buzzer to the suite sounded. The dress he had ordered for her, no doubt. He swallowed a swear word. While she'd been in the bathroom, he'd decided he wanted more than a few minutes with her. He'd arranged for a delayed delivery for the dress, ordered the meal, cancelled his plans for the late afternoon and evening. Now his snatched time with her had run out. Fantasies of spending more minutes, more hours with her clamoured at him. But the reality of his situation dictated he had to usher her out of his hotel room with no further delay.

'Aren't you going to let them in?' she said, still holding his gaze. 'It might be the dress you ordered for me.'

He wanted to send the delivery person away. Keep her here with him, alluring in the black velvet dressing gown. But she had to leave, and she needed the dress before she could do so. 'Of course,' he said and reluctantly rose to accept the delivery.

He returned with a boutique bag that bore an exclusive, instantly recognisable label.

Ms Mermaid's eyebrows rose. 'You chose well,' she said.

'My sister has good taste,' he said.

His guest got up from the table and stepped away from it to meet him in the open space of the living room. He held out the boutique's bag to her. But she made no move to take it from his hands.

Instead she looked up at him and took a deep breath that made the lapels of her gown part further to reveal more than a glimpse of the curves of her breasts. He had to force himself not to let his gaze drift in that direction.

'I don't want to take the dress,' she said. 'If I do, I have to go. And I don't want to go. Not… not yet.' The stumble over her final words made Edward see she wasn't as boldly confident as she seemed. So she felt it too—this inexplicable connection. Elation surged through him.

'I don't want you to go,' he said, speaking the unvarnished truth. But what he wanted wasn't always possible. His royal birth had brought with it incredible privilege but also responsibility and duty.

She took a step closer. 'Then…then should I not stay?'

The air between them hummed with anticipation and shimmered with unspoken words. Her lovely mouth parted and she swayed towards him in an invitation that was impossible to resist. With a groan, Edward stepped closer. His eyes stayed locked with hers as his mouth came down on hers. Her lips were soft and warm and sweet under his and, as he pulled her to him, he pushed aside every reason why he should not be kissing her.

* * *

Sally didn't know what she'd been expecting when she'd invited his kiss, but it wasn't this instant ignition of long dormant passion. Desire flamed through her, urgent and demanding, as his lips possessed hers, his tongue tangled with hers in intimate exploration. She trembled from the overwhelming force of her reaction, pressed her body closer to his, strained to be closer to hard muscular chest, strong thighs.

At this moment he was everything she wanted, everything she *needed*. She wound her arms around his neck as she kissed him back, demanding more. He deepened the kiss, hard and hungry.

Her wants, her needs had been put on hold for so achingly long. There had been no hugs, no kisses, no *intimacy* in her life even before she finished with the actor. And it would be the same when she got back to London. Running her business, with its demanding clients and team of creatives, always looking for the next innovation that would keep Sally Harrington Interiors on top, used up every scrap of energy and drive. But then she'd had to dig deep to find even more of herself to deal with the new demands on top of her business, brought about by her older brother's sudden return. The refurbishing of the Harrington Park was a full-time job in itself, the roof garden another. Something had to give. And her needs had been pushed right to the back of the line. Until now. Now her body was clamouring for its turn.

As she revelled in the sensations of the moment, Sally blocked everything else but this gorgeous man and how he made her feel. Her family tragedies, her conflict about her older brother's return, the pressure of the deadline to restore the hotel, her empty, lonely personal life were shoved firmly to the back of her mind. All she wanted was the pleasure of his kiss, the aching anticipation of more. She needed this escape from the reality of her Ice Queen life. She *deserved* it. He slid his hands down her back. She gasped at the intense sensation of his touch, her awareness she was wearing nothing at all under the robe.

She would take the escape he was offering.

At her gasp, he stilled and broke the kiss. She gave an unintelligible whimper of distress at the withdrawal of his warmth—she had no breath for anything more.

He tilted her chin upward with his fingers, so she looked up into his face. His gaze was intent, his voice unsteady. 'Is this what you want?'

She didn't need him to explain what *this* meant. Wordlessly, she nodded.

'Because if it isn't you need to go. Now.'

She replied without hesitation. 'I want this. I want *you*.' This was pure, primal need.

'I want you too. But...but this is all it can be.'

She took a deep breath to steady herself. 'Are you married? Because, if so, I can't—' Despite her past with unattainable men, married men were strictly out of bounds.

'I'm not married,' he said. 'But there are... other reasons why I can't give you anything more than one night.'

Sally felt swept by a glorious sense of freedom, of chains falling away—the self-imposed constrictions on her tightly controlled life. *A one-night stand.* She had never done anything remotely like it. But she had never wanted a man like she wanted this man.

She could pick up the dress, go change in the bathroom, walk out—and always wonder what it would have been like to be with him. Or she could take what he offered—and gift him the same. No past. No future. No strings.

And no regrets.

'One night it is,' she said with a shiver of exhilaration and anticipation.

There would be no anxiety about tomorrow. No possibility of an ill-fated relationship spluttering to an acrimonious end.

Just one night.

All she had to do was release her inhibitions and heed the reckless call to sensual adventure.

He looked serious. 'So long as you're sure. I don't want to take advantage of your near drowning, your shock—'

'You're not taking advantage of me.' She stepped closer to him, rested her hands on his shoulders, looked up at him with a slow smile. 'Perhaps I'm taking advantage of you.'

He smiled back and she was struck again how much she liked that smile. How much she liked *him*.

'I hadn't thought of it in those terms.'

That voice!

'So…let's not waste one second of our one night together,' she murmured.

His eyes searched her face. 'I wasn't expecting this,' he said slowly.

'Neither was I. But…but I'm glad it's happening.'

'Me too.'

He laughed and pulled her close. She pressed her lips to his. Ice Queen? *Huh*. She was melting with need. For him.

He kissed her back. This time she sensed he held nothing back, his lips urgent and demanding.

Heaven.

Very soon kissing was no longer enough. She craved so much more. With impatient fingers, she tugged his shirt from his trousers, slid her hands to his back—smooth, warm skin over rippling muscle—as he groaned his appreciation. She broke their kiss just long enough to push his shirt up and over his head.

'We need to even the score here,' he said, his voice husky. He kissed a trail from the corner of her mouth, down the column of her throat to the curve of her breast, meanwhile undoing the sash of her robe. 'I'm wondering what underwear you have on under there.'

'Wh-why not find out?' she managed to stutter.

He pushed the velvet robe off her shoulders. Her nipples tightened and tingled under his appreciative gaze. 'No bra. As I thought.' She wondered when he had actually thought that but was too caught up in the sensation of his hands on her bare skin to actually ask. When he caressed her breasts she could think of nothing else and could only gasp when he followed his hands with his mouth, licking and teasing her nipples. Desire pooled deep in her belly.

The front of her robe slid further open to reveal her bare thighs. 'Aren't you going to check if I'm wearing panties?'

He cleared his throat. 'I think we should take this to the bedroom.'

Effortlessly, he picked her up. 'You're very strong,' she gasped as she looped her arms around his neck and pressed into his hard chest. She was five foot ten and it would be no mean feat to lift her. Normally she would bridle at such a masterful tactic, but she loved the way he took charge. His strength made her feel feminine and desired. It wouldn't be something she'd care for in real life, but this wasn't real life. This was more akin to fantasy.

'Fastest way to get you to the bed,' he said in a voice that set her senses rioting.

There seemed to be a number of bedrooms in the suite but he carried her to what must be his; she recognised the spicy scent of his soap from the adjoining bathroom. An enormous bed loomed ahead of her, piled with silk cushions. But her hotelier's eye was switched off. She didn't give a toss about the furnishings. Only him and the sensual intent in his dark eyes.

He pushed the robe right off her shoulders. There was a moment's awkwardness as her elbow got stuck and he had to help her extract her arms from the sleeves. Laughter bubbled from them both at her predicament. Laughing with him was almost as arousing as anything he did with his clever mouth and fingers. The velvet fell off her body in a silky slide and pooled at her feet. As she stepped out of it, she felt self-conscious about her nakedness. But then came the liberating thought that it didn't matter. She wouldn't see him again. Wasn't that part of the fantasy? She straightened her shoulders and let herself bask in the sensual caress of his eyes.

They tumbled together onto the bed to land facing each other, kissing distance apart. Her breath quickened, as did his. She took a few heartbeats to admire him, the defined muscles of his chest and arms, his six-pack. He was the most gorgeous man she'd ever seen. And there was so much more for her to admire. She reached to undo his belt. 'Now it's my turn to even the score,' she murmured.

More laughter ensued as he helped her remove his remaining clothes and toss them on the floor. Then the laughter stilled as she faced him with no barriers whatsoever between them. Her heart was beating so loud she felt sure he could hear it. He reached out for her and traced the contours of her face in gentle exploration. She trembled at his touch. Tentatively, she did the same, his skin smooth under her exploring fingers as she traced along his high cheekbones, his straight, narrow nose, his full, sexy mouth. His expression was a mix of puzzlement and awe, as if he couldn't believe she was here in his bed with him. Something made her wonder if he were as unfamiliar with the code for a no-strings fling as she was.

They spent a long time exploring each other's bodies. He learned just what it took to please her and arouse her to the point where she couldn't wait a second longer for him to enter her. She whimpered as she strained her body towards him.

He pulled her close so they were skin to skin, feminine curves against male hardness. She bucked her hips towards him, letting him know how ready she was for him. But, as he positioned himself, she put her hand on his cheek to stay him. There was something she felt compelled to say before the ultimate intimacy. 'My name is Sally,' she whispered.

'Edward,' he said, his voice hoarse.

After that, she didn't think of anything else but the intensity of their lovemaking. She was so aroused she climaxed almost as soon as he entered her. The world shrank to just him and her in the luxurious bedroom high above the city of Singapore. Nothing had prepared her for the storm of pleasure as they concentrated on discovering what pleased each other. There was no more laughter, just murmurs of pleasure, sighs and cries of fulfilment. On her third climax she couldn't help a tear from escaping the corner of her eye. He frowned and tenderly wiped it away. 'It's nothing,' she whispered. 'Don't stop.'

Her tears were for the realisation that she

would never again have the chance to experience this intense fulfilment with him.

No regrets, she fiercely reminded herself. Perhaps it was so perfect *because* it was only for the one night.

Insomnia had plagued her since her older brother's return. She was too wired from worry about whether the tattered remnants of their once happy family could be woven into something new and strong. But now, replete, she drifted towards a deep sleep with her rescuer's—*Edward's*—arm slung across her.

When she awoke it was well past midnight, according to the clock glowing on the nightstand. The myriad lights of Singapore twinkled through the floor-to-ceiling windows. For a moment she didn't know where she was and looked around the room in momentary panic. Then she remembered and smiled. A beautiful man slept next to her on his back, the linen sheet rumpled over his hips. Edward—if that was indeed his name. His breathing was deep and even, his face heartbreakingly handsome in repose, dark stubble shadowing his jaw. She ached to kiss him lightly on his lips, thank him, whisper her goodbye.

But she couldn't risk waking him. The awkwardness that would surely follow would be unbearable. She'd never done this before. Perhaps there was an etiquette to be followed after a one-night stand with a stranger. If so, she hadn't read the rule book. The best thing she could think of to do was to leave without any fuss. They'd agreed on one night. He'd had his reasons for setting the limit; she'd had hers for accepting it. It had been the most glorious one night. In fact, every moment with him had been memorable, from when he'd fished her out of the pool, to eating *dim sum,* to sharing passion like she'd never known existed.

The thawing of the Ice Queen.

She was grateful to him more than he could know. *No regrets.*

She slid as silently as she could to the edge of the bed. He murmured something in his sleep, in a language she didn't understand. She froze. But then his breathing returned to the steady rhythm of a deep sleep.

She stepped over the discarded velvet robe, his clothes tossed nearby. Then tiptoed to the door of his bedroom. She turned back just the once to blow him the most silent of kisses. Then crept away.

Hastily, as silently as she could, she opened the boutique bag to find an elegant straw-coloured linen dress that bore the label of a famous Italian designer. It was a perfect fit and fell modestly below the knee, which was a good thing as she was without underwear. There was a pair of designer open-back sandals in the bag too. They were a little on the small side, but she was grateful for them. She would slip them on once she was out of the suite and headed down to the hotel lobby. Then she'd catch a taxi back to her own hotel.

Sally found the bathroom and stuffed her own wet clothes and shoes into a hotel laundry bag to take with her. Inside her small handbag, she heard her phone ping with a message. She stilled, fearful the sound would wake her lover. But there was no sound from Edward's bedroom.

Carefully, she reached for the phone and found several missed messages from her twin, Jay. She would call him later, when she could speak coherently. The unanswered calls could be blamed on the time zones. Jay would understand. She and her twin were opposites in personality, he the outgoing one people flocked to, she the more introverted one who found it difficult to trust people enough to open up to them. Jay was the sunshine to her shadow. But they'd always been on the same wavelength in that special way that twins, even fraternal ones, could be.

But she wouldn't tell anyone, even Jay, about Edward. Or indeed anything that had happened after she'd fallen into the pool. Edward would remain her private secret to hug to herself. No one would ever know about the night where she had scaled the peaks of sensual ecstasy with a handsome stranger.

Edward awoke at dawn to a cold, empty bed. Immediately he realised he was alone and was overwhelmed by a deep sense of loss. He reached out a hand to find sheets still with a hint of her warmth, her scent.

Sally.

He suspected she was long gone. But he threw himself out of bed to check the rest of the suite. The only trace of her ever having been there was the carefully folded tissue paper sitting next to the empty boutique bag. Nothing in her bathroom save the lingering scent of the body wash she'd used. He breathed it in, but it did nothing to ease his sense of loss. He cradled his head in his hands and groaned.

Why had he let her go?

The answer came to him with stark clarity, almost as if it were his father the King intoning the words.

Because of your duty to the throne and your people.

She had done him a favour by slipping away in the dark. Her actions had spared him—and her—the awkwardness of a morning-after encounter. He could give no glib promises that he could keep in touch or they would meet again. The truth was he was destined to marry in a loveless political union.

He had only the memories of an amazing woman with whom he'd shared unforgettable lovemaking and a connection that went so much deeper than the sexual. That kind of connection was rare. Instinct told him that, if nurtured, what he had shared with her could grow into something profound. But he could never see that connection flourish. The one night was all he could ever have with her.

Sally. It was a common enough English name.

He could track her down if he was so inclined. Access to the hotel's CCTV cameras would be easy—after all his family owned this hotel. He could note the licence plate of the taxi she would no doubt have taken. Then trace it to her hotel. But that would put him in no less of an untenable position. He should be grateful for that brief time he had shared with her.

Still, he was haunted by the melancholic thought that he had let go something—*someone*—more precious than the egg-sized rubies and emeralds in the ceremonial crown that would one day be placed on his head when he was crowned King.

CHAPTER THREE

Five weeks later

SALLY HAD FLOWN to Mumbai last week, Dubai the week before and before that made a quick trip to Tokyo for a briefing on the restoration of a small but significant castle. In between trips she'd been flat out working in London. Jet lag was piling up on jet lag with never a chance to get over it. Now early December saw her in Singapore again, five weeks after her first visit, having flown eight hours direct from Japan's Narita Airport after a brief site visit to the castle. She'd arrived very late the previous night and hadn't been able to sleep either on the plane or at her destination. No wonder she was so exhausted.

The fatigue was overwhelming, bringing with it nausea and insomnia worse than she had ever suffered. She threw herself back on her hotel bed in a desperate effort to get some rest before her lunchtime meeting. It wasn't the historic hotel she'd stayed in last visit. Nor was it the sky-high hotel with the rooftop garden where she had spent the most memorable night of her life. Memorable in the true sense of the word—she had been unable to forget the man who'd called himself Edward.

It hadn't been as easy as she'd so blithely anticipated to put that night behind her. Not just the sensational lovemaking but also how much she'd enjoyed his company—in and out of bed. A day didn't go by that she didn't think about him. She couldn't count the number of times her heart had jolted when she'd seen a tall Asian man on the streets of London, only to find up close he looked nothing like her one-time lover.

She'd felt a connection with Edward like she'd never felt before and couldn't help but wish she'd been able to explore it. But she'd gone into their encounter with eyes open. *One night.* That was the agreement. And she didn't regret it, not for a moment. Letting go of her strict self-control, unleashing her inhibitions, learning what intense pleasure lovemaking could bring when you were with the right person, had done her good. Now she knew to what heights the Ice Queen could soar.

Trouble was, how could another man ever live up to him?

No wonder she couldn't forget him.

She adjusted the pillow and forced herself to focus on work, the reason she was here again in Singapore. When she'd got home from her first trip to Singapore, she'd asked for a meeting in the boardroom with her brothers Jay and Hugo. The idea for the urban roof garden had been Hugo's. In a spirited discussion, Sally had expressed her concerns about the practicality of such a venture. 'Lush green outdoor roof gardens are all very well in a tropical climate like Singapore,' she'd said. 'But how successful would something on that scale be in the middle of an English winter? I know there are such gardens in London, but we want something unique. Palm trees and exotic blooms simply don't feel right for the Harrington brand and our relaunch. I propose something different.'

Hugo had protested. She'd learned her older brother had strong views; he was now the owner of a very successful chain of boutique hotels in the United States. He was used to his opinions being taken as law.

'Let me outline my alternative,' she'd said,

using every skill she'd learned in dealing with difficult clients in her own business. 'I didn't just visit rooftop gardens when I was in Singapore. I also saw the most amazing climate-controlled indoor gardens. The Changi Airport has an indoor forest complete with indoor waterfall. Wouldn't an enclosed garden be a better option in our climate? Why not an indoor winter wonderland? A splendid mini forest with fir trees, winter berry shrubs, snow and a skating rink that looks like a frozen lake. It would be perfect for an English Christmas. And what an incredible space to hold our Christmas Eve launch party for the restored Harrington Park.'

Hugo had frowned while Jay had given her an encouraging thumbs-up from behind his brother's back. 'Where would you put such a garden?' Hugo had said.

'The hotel roof would need an incredible amount of reinforcement that's simply not possible in our timeframe. The large covered courtyard to the north of the entrance foyer is essentially unused, and the gardens have been neglected. Our winter wonderland, enclosed with glass walls and roof, could rejuvenate that under-utilised space. After the holiday season we could convert it to a beautiful conservatory with glamorous outdoor furniture and potted plants appropriate to the season. Then bring back the winter garden the following year as a highlight of the Harrington Park holiday calendar.'

She'd paused, out of breath from the effort of injecting a high level of enthusiasm to her proposal.

'It's worth considering,' Hugo had said slowly.

'Oh, and another thing,' she'd said, her voice breaking a little. 'The winter garden could be a memorial to our parents. Daddy loved Christmas and, if you remember, winter was Mummy's favourite season.'

'Great idea,' Jay had said.

Hugo had blanched and Sally had clenched her fists under the table. Had she gone too far with her idea for the memorial? All those years ago, Hugo had taken off to America and abandoned his mother and siblings. However, Hugo seemed to believe *they* had abandoned *him*. He was bitter about their mother; Sally couldn't help but be defensive on her behalf. Yet in Sally's dealings so far with her newfound brother she'd found him to be scrupulously fair.

On that first visit to Singapore she'd met with

a leading Singapore landscape architect, Oscar Yeo, responsible for some of the indoor gardens that had so impressed her. He had referred her to his associated London office, who also had expertise in working with artificial snow. With their expert input she had come up with a detailed timeline for the winter wonderland and had been able to slide it across the table to Hugo.

Her computer-assisted drawings had shown him exactly how it would look. Hugo had almost immediately approved her plan. The landscape architects had been engaged and a project manager appointed. Now, five weeks later, thanks to a team of experienced professionals who'd pulled out all the stops, work was well under way on the winter garden.

But there had been a few hiccups that threatened to delay completion by Christmas Eve. They *had* to meet that deadline. She'd always found it better to deal face to face with such problems rather than relying on phone calls and emails. Hence her flight to Singapore and her scheduled lunchtime meeting with Oscar Yeo. There was also something nagging at her about the plan, a detail that she had perhaps overlooked, but she couldn't think quite what it might be.

Her exhaustion was bone-deep. But, her mind racing, Sally found it impossible to rest. She got up from the bed, too quickly it seemed, as she suddenly felt overwhelmed by dizziness. She clutched onto the bedhead for support and waited until the room stopped spinning around her. As she took a deep breath to steady herself, she was hit by a sudden rush of nausea so urgent she barely made it to the bathroom on time. The bout left her feeling weak and shaky. Food poisoning. Was it something she'd eaten on the plane? Or maybe she'd caught a horrid stomach flu? Great. Just what she didn't need right now with such a busy schedule. She was booked to fly home to London the following day.

After a long shower, she felt a little better. The hotel was on Orchard Road, Singapore's famous shopping strip. There was an underground mall beneath the hotel. She'd head down and get some anti-nausea medication from the pharmacy. It was important to be on top of things for the meeting with the landscape architect.

From her suitcase she pulled out a full-skirted sundress she hadn't worn since her last trip here in early November. Surprisingly, it was too tight across the bust. It must have shrunk, although it had been carefully laundered. She tried a button-through shirt and a skirt. Again, too tight. She swore under her breath. How had this happened? It wasn't the clothes; it was her. She didn't have large breasts but suddenly they seemed a size larger. How could that be?

She sat down rather too quickly in the hotel armchair. Swollen, tender breasts. Nausea and fatigue. It couldn't be. No. *She couldn't possibly be pregnant.* Impossible. There had only been that time with Edward. She wiped her hand across her suddenly damp forehead. Just one time was enough to get pregnant—and there had been more than one time. She was on the pill. She'd told him that when he'd mentioned protection. But the pill she was on had to be taken at the same time every day and never missed. With her erratic timetable, regularly crossing time zones and out of routine, it would be easy enough to miss a pill or two.

With hands that weren't steady she threw on a light embroidered kaftan—at least that fitted—and headed down to the pharmacy. Her thoughts were running away too fast. Methodical as she was, she bought three different types of pregnancy testing kit. They would prove she wasn't pregnant.

All three of the testers indicated that she was, indeed, pregnant. She stared, stunned, at the results. The testers could be faulty. Did the pharmacist have any other brands she could try? But deep in her heart she knew three testers were a good enough sample.

She was pregnant.

About five weeks pregnant, she thought as she frantically counted back to the glorious night with Edward. So much for a fling without consequences.

She paced up and down the room until she got dizzy again.

How could she have let this happen?

Her first urge was to call Jay; at one time he had always been the first person with whom she shared momentous news or asked for advice. But she resisted. She had to handle this on her own. Besides, Jay had his own issues with Chloe, his teenage love with whom he had recently reconnected. She hoped all was well; she'd liked his schoolmate. But Chloe had broken her brother's heart the first time around. She would have to contend with Sally if she broke it again.

Panic paralysed her. She couldn't have a baby on her own. Children had been on the distant agenda for when she got married. *If* she got married, that was. Her lack of luck with men had made her begin to think she wasn't the marrying kind.

She wasn't exactly surrounded by happy marriages. She'd been bridesmaid to her two closest friends from school. They were both already divorced. Her parents' marriage had been happy although, as her father had died suddenly of a heart attack when she'd been only six years old, she would hardly have noticed if it hadn't been. Just a year after being widowed, her mother had married Nick Wolfe, an American businessman who had been a regular visitor to the hotel. Nick had been all sunshine and unicorns until he'd got a ring on her mother's finger. Things hadn't been so romantic when the honeymoon was over. Sally suspected her mother's second marriage had been anything but perfect. As well, it had ushered in the decline of the Harrington Park Hotel.

She was almost glad her mother wasn't here to see the predicament her daughter had got herself into. Pregnant to a stranger after a one-night stand. She didn't know the father's surname, or even if his first name was real. How irresponsible did that sound? She shut her eyes tight at the thought of what her brothers would think. And yet…this baby had been conceived in joy, no matter how temporary. The father was considerate and kind and had made her laugh as well as shared with her the best sex of her life. She could only think well of him.

She didn't need to be married to be a mother. Twenty-seven was biologically an excellent age to have a baby. She owned a successful, profitable business and her own home. Her spacious period apartment in South Kensington had been bought with the first part of her inheritance from her maternal grandmother when she was twenty-one. The second part of the substantial inheritance had kicked in when she was twenty-five. She could afford the best for her baby.

Her baby.

She placed her hand on her still flat tummy. Such a new thought and already not such a terrifying one.

She could do this.

But she had to push her pregnancy worries aside—she was good at suppressing inconvenient emotion—and concentrate on her meeting with the landscape architect. Fortunately, the linen shift dress she'd brought with her for the meeting was loosely cut across the bust and still fitted. So did the matching lightweight jacket. She'd learned from her last visit to Singapore that while it might be sweltering outside, air conditioning inside could be chilly.

She'd chosen her hotel because it was only a block from the office tower where Oscar Yeo's company had its headquarters. The heat and humidity hit her as she stepped out of the hotel onto the busy street. She halted, stunned.

So many Christmas decorations.

If she'd thought she could escape Christmas while in Singapore she'd been mistaken. Orchard Road was known as the Oxford Street of Singapore and the spectacular festive decorations rivalled anything she might see in London. To see Christmas cheer in a hot, sunny December was disorientating. It was so different from seeing decorations in gloomy, wintry London when it got dark by four p.m. and showed the illuminations to their best advantage.

However, none of the Christmas bling impressed her. Buskers playing Christmas carols

grated on her ears. She'd become very bah hum-
bug about Christmas.

It hadn't always been that way. When she was a
child, with both adored parents alive, they'd lived
in their beautiful family home in the grounds of
the Harrington Park Hotel. It had been the estate manager's house in the days the hotel was
a grand private home. Christmas Eve had been
the major celebration for the hotel, but her parents had made it about family too. Her memories were childish ones, her impressions of love
and magic and the fabulous Christmas tree in
the hotel lobby that had towered above her. Each
year, she and her two brothers would be allowed
to buy a special ornament each to hang on the
tree, and their parents hung one too.

One of her clearest memories was of her father, jovial and kind, lifting her up in his arms
to hang her ornament as high on the tree as she
could reach. She had felt safe, secure, loved. That
had been the last Christmas her father had been
alive. She had never felt that loved again. And
Christmas had lost its sparkle. Their mother had
done her best to maintain the festive traditions,
but her heart hadn't been in it.

When her mother had married Nick she'd

handed over the reins of the Harrington Park to her new husband so she could spend more time with her children. He had immediately made drastic changes and had set about chipping away at the Harrington traditions, including those long-standing Christmas customs that he had deemed a waste of money. First to go had been the Christmas Eve party. An enormous tree, decorated with the family heirlooms, had never gone up in the lobby again.

Sally had been too young to be aware of all that, just that her life had changed irrevocably. Hugo, however, seven years older than Sally, had grown up with the expectation that he would one day run the family hotel. He was only too aware of what had happened. When she and Jay had met their older brother again after seventeen years' absence, he'd told them that it was Nick Wolfe who had forced him out of the hotel and their lives. Nick, thief of their legacy, who had mismanaged the hotel so badly that he'd had to declare bankruptcy and sell.

Hugo was determined to reverse that. One of the first things her older brother had done when he'd corralled her and Jay into working with him on the restoration of the hotel was to go through the meticulously kept archives of the hotel. The idea had been to show them what a grand hotel the Harrington Park had been before its decline and to inspire them to do even better.

All three had delighted at the images of the splendid balls, the many famous celebrities and dignitaries who had stayed in the hotel in its heyday. There were also priceless records of the practical running of the hotel, although no such records had been kept under their stepfather's management.

Jay, an award-winning chef with his own Michelin starred restaurant, had been excited about the old menus from days gone by and had decided to recreate some of them, while adding his own twist. He'd employed his friend, Louis Joubert, from Paris as head chef to work with him.

Sally's particular interest was the décor of both the guestrooms and the public spaces. A real find had been invoices from years ago for the traditional porcelain bathtubs and basins in the bathrooms, and the subsequent discovery that the firm was still in business. That kind of hardware was as important as the luxurious furnishings and fabrics she was splashing out on. Her attention to such practical details as well as the wow of the decorating was part of her success as a designer.

Then there had been the photos of the Christmas Eve party for family, guests and staff—dating right back to the nineteen-twenties. She and her brothers had fallen silent, each swamped by their own memories. Sally could barely bring herself to look at the images for that last Christmas when her father had been alive. When they'd been a happy, united family.

Christmas celebrations after Hugo left had comprised just Sally, Jay and her mother. Not even Nick Wolfe, who'd had no time for family celebrations. Her grandmother had refused to come anywhere near the hotel once Nick had come on the scene. After their mother had died in a car accident when Sally was thirteen, she'd stopped celebrating Christmas at all.

Now Hugo was determined to restore the Christmas Eve traditions in all their grandeur with a spectacular reopening party. And time was running out to get the winter wonderland finished.

Sally walked as quickly as she could in the heat and humidity of Singapore to her destination, shunning the gigantic Christmas tree that was the centrepiece of the Orchard Road decorations. As she passed a newsstand a magazine poster caught her eye. It featured a strikingly handsome black-haired man who looked very much like Edward. Her heart jolted and she stopped in her tracks to stare at it, then made herself move on before she even read the coverlines. When would she ever stop thinking she saw the man at every turn? She would *never* be able to forget him, that was for sure. Always, she would wonder about the father of her child.

Her meeting with Oscar Yeo went well. She hadn't dared eat lunch; even to push food around her plate made her feel queasy. The technical and production issues were solved to her satisfaction. Now she had every confidence her winter wonderland would come in on time and under budget. The trip to Singapore had been worth it; she could confidently fly back to London tomorrow and report to Hugo on a successful trip.

As she made her farewells to Oscar, who was both professional and courteous, he asked whether he and his wife could include her in their evening's entertainment and show her more of Singapore. Although she appreciated the gesture, Sally politely declined. She was desperate to get back to the hotel. She'd planned to use her afternoon to revisit some of the indoor gardens but that had to be put on hold. Much as she loved the design for the winter wonderland, there was something missing that continued to elude her and she'd hoped to find further inspiration. But she badly needed rest and time to give more thought to how she would manage the changes her unexpected pregnancy would bring to her life.

On the way back to her hotel, however, she couldn't resist popping into an upscale baby store, just one of the many glitzy shops on Orchard Road, to buy a darling little baby cardigan that cost an inordinate amount of Singapore dollars. Holding it, she felt stirrings of excitement and wonder.

She was going to have a baby.

Her other shopping expedition was to a convenience store to buy a packet of dry crackers. Once back in the hotel, she lay back on the bed in the blissful air conditioning, nibbled on the crackers and sipped fizzy mineral water until her tummy settled. She used the remote to turn on the television.

It opened to an English-speaking news service. Singapore was a vibrant, progressive city state, one of the leading financial centres of the world. Sally had seen it described as an alpha-plus global city, and the local news issues interested her. It was an excellent place for her to do business as English seemed to be the first language. One news item ended and another began. An image of yet another Edward lookalike appeared on the screen. Having just discovered she was pregnant with his baby was making her think way too much about him without all these lookalike reminders. She went to flick the television off but then suddenly jerked forward, her mineral water splashing on the bedcover without her even noticing.

She stared, mesmerised, as a different newsreader chattered on.

'Rumours are growing that Asia's most eligible—and hottest!—bachelor, thirty-one-year-old Prince Edward of Tianlipin, is about to announce his long-awaited engagement. The Crown Prince of the wealthy island kingdom has been tantalising us with his tight-lipped "No comment". Yet his Singapore house has been completely refurbished. Getting it ready for his future bride? Could it be the lucky lady is from Singapore?'

The TV showed a montage of pictures of the Prince: serious in a business suit, elegant in a tuxedo, smiling in white shorts on the deck of a yacht and, most mindboggling of all, solemn in the ceremonial national dress of his country, heavily encrusted with gold and precious stones.

Sally froze as she stared at the screen. In one film clip he held up his hand as if to say *No comment*. The voice was immediately recognisable. So was that devastating smile. She reeled at the revelation, her heart pounding so hard she shook, and her breath came in short, panicky gasps. She put her hand to her heart to steady herself. There could be no doubt. It was him. Edward. *Prince* Edward.

Suddenly the father of her baby had a name and identity. Sally uttered a strangled, mirthless laugh. When it came to unattainable men, she sure knew how to pick them. A prince. An about-to-be-engaged prince. A celebrity prince, no less.

But she had been attracted to him as just a regular businessman, she thought wistfully. He'd seemed her equal.

The newsreader continued. 'Prince Edward will be attending the charity gala at the Beauville Hotel this evening. Rumour informs us he will be attending solo. There's no doubt about it—Prince Edward is holding his romance cards very close to his chest.'

That news segment finished; Sally switched off the television. Immediately, with hands that weren't steady, she turned on her laptop to research Crown Prince Edward of Tianlipin.

She discovered his home was a substantial island in the South China sea, north-east of Singapore and south of Vietnam. Tianlipin was a hereditary monarchy and, while staggeringly rich in oil and gas, in modern times its fastest growing export was telecommunications. Billionaire Crown Prince Edward had been educated in both his home country and Singapore, with postgraduate studies at Cambridge and Harvard. He was CEO of the family owned telecommunications company and spent considerable time in Singapore. His sister Princess Jennifer ran the family's international hotel portfolio, which included the Singapore hotel with the rooftop resort.

Slowly Sally closed her laptop. No wonder his sister was so familiar with the hotel boutique. And that was why Edward had occupied what had seemed to be the presidential suite. Looking back, she realised he had been as keen to keep away from unwanted attention as she had been. After all, he was considered to be *Asia's hottest bachelor.*

He must have women by the thousands flinging themselves at him. She'd been just one more, she thought a little bitterly. One more before he got engaged. But she refused to let her thoughts go in that direction. He had not set out to seduce her; she had made the first move. He had been at pains to ensure he wasn't taking advantage of her shocked state after her near drowning. Their lovemaking had been completely consensual, and he had treated her with respect and consideration. Would she have gone ahead if he had told her the truth about his identity? Most likely not. Firstly, she probably wouldn't have believed him, and secondly, if she had, she would have been too intimidated by his royal status to let him kiss her, let alone undo the tie of her robe.

Then she wouldn't have had that memorable night with him. Then she wouldn't be pregnant with his child. She sighed a long, heartfelt sigh. The revelation of his true identity made her predicament so much more complicated. And completely smashed any lingering hope that she might bump into him somewhere in Singapore and discover he missed her as much as she missed him. Because wasn't it the truth that, deep down in the frozen heart she had allowed him to warm for just one night, that hope was the real reason she had jumped at the chance to return to Singapore?

Now she knew who he really was, it would be possible to get in touch with him. But she cringed at the thought. How would he see such contact? An anonymous one-night stand showing up in Singapore, pregnant and demanding money from a prince? Sally shuddered at what she imagined his reaction might be. She didn't need his millions—no, it was billions. She certainly didn't need the humiliation. But did he deserve to know he was going to be a father?

She was more than capable of bringing up her baby on her own and she intended to do just that. Her child would have the security of one loving parent who would put him or her first. Boy or girl? She hadn't yet thought about it, but the image of an adorable little black-haired, brown-eyed boy looking very like his father flashed into her thoughts. A little boy—or a little black-haired girl—who would one day ask questions about his or her father. And if she hadn't told Edward about the child's existence she would have to lie.

All of a sudden, her situation seemed utterly overwhelming. She prided herself on keeping control of her emotions, locking down weakness and acting the Ice Queen when it came to revealing hurt. She'd learned those survival techniques when, at the age of thirteen, grieving for her mother, her stepfather had dropped all pretence of caring for his stepchildren. He'd made her and Jay full boarders at their school, effectively keeping them away from everything and everyone they'd known for weeks at a time. And left them to fend for themselves.

Now she was feeling more vulnerable than she had ever imagined she could feel. With brutal honesty, she forced herself to face the truth. Edward, the man she had thought she would never see again, was in Singapore—and she desperately wanted to see him. Not force a meeting. Not tell him she was carrying his baby. Just see him, even from afar. Perhaps just to prove to herself he was real.

While she was guilty of prevaricating on emotion, Sally was good at making snap decisions.

She picked up her phone and dialled Oscar Yeo's number. She asked him if it would be possible for him to get her a ticket for the charity gala event being held at the Beauville Hotel that night.

He did better than that. He and his wife were attending the gala themselves. They already had a ticket for their daughter, but she'd cried off. Sally would be more than welcome to come with him and his wife. She could sit at their table. They would pick her up from her hotel.

Sally spluttered her thanks. Then got herself in a totally uncharacteristic tizz. What on earth would she wear?

CHAPTER FOUR

A KNOT OF tension settled in Sally's chest the moment she entered the ornate ballroom of the Beauville Hotel with Oscar Yeo and his delightful lawyer wife Iris. *Where was Edward?* She had to force herself to act composed and not peer around the crowded room, anxiously seeking a glimpse of the Prince. She was on a razor-edge of anticipation and dread—what if he was not as she remembered? That edge was only too close to leading to a plummet of despair—what if he wasn't there at all? The thought she might come close to him and he wouldn't recognise her didn't bear thinking about.

The other women at the gala were dressed to the hilt in formal gowns and an abundance of jewellery. Thank heaven she had decided against the simple black cocktail dress she kept packed to cover any social occasions she might encounter on her frequent business trips. Instead, after her phone call with Oscar, she'd ventured out again to Orchard Road and found something more glamorous in one of the designer boutiques.

Disconcertingly, the assistant at the store had known immediately she was pregnant but had thought her further along than five weeks. However, there could be no mistake about the timing of conception. There had been no one else but Edward. When she'd asked the assistant how she knew, the woman had replied that years of observing female bodies in changing rooms meant she could just tell.

Did that mean others could tell? For how long could she conceal her pregnancy? When would she tell Jay and Hugo they were going to be uncles? What would she say about the father of her baby? Her doubts and fears strangled rational thought. She couldn't consider all that just now. The possibility of seeing Edward was the only thought she wanted to occupy her mind.

If she did see him—and he saw her—she felt confident in the elegantly cut long gown in midnight-blue silk, embellished with swirls of beading in shades of indigo through violet. She'd bought new sky-high heels in a toning dark shade of blue, deciding she might as well enjoy heels while she still could, before her pregnancy meant she had to graduate to flats. Luckily, she'd snagged the last appointment of the afternoon with the hairdresser in the hotel, who'd put up her hair in a stylish knot. She thought back to when all she had to wear was a black velvet dressing gown, and still she'd wanted to look her best for Edward.

She went to accept a cocktail from a waiter passing drinks around on a silver tray, then remembered she now shouldn't be drinking alcohol and swapped it for a soft drink. Feeling more on edge by the second, she stuck close by her hosts as she didn't know one other person. Except Edward, of course. And could she say she really knew him at all?

She followed Oscar and Iris to their table, set about a third of the way down the expansive room. Thankfully, the other people on the table were from Oscar's company, and they were all intrigued by the winter wonderland garden at the Harrington Park. Social chit-chat wasn't Sally's strength, especially when her mind was elsewhere with a tall, black-haired prince, but she could always talk fluently and happily about work.

Of course, she didn't indicate to any of her

table companions that she had any interest whatsoever in Crown Prince Edward of Tianlipin. But he was an almost immediate topic of conversation. The Prince was guest of honour at the gala in aid of a cancer research institute—an important donor, it seemed. But it wasn't his philanthropy that had Iris Yeo agog with interest; rather it was the rumour and speculation about his impending engagement.

It took a mammoth effort for Sally to appear impartial, to express interest in the Prince without going overboard—even though she was dying to find out everything she possibly could about him. Especially his engagement, the thought of which made her feel the ache of a deep, stabbing envy.

Singapore was one of the world's most expensive cities, with many ultra-wealthy people, Iris explained, but this man was a real-life *prince.* His kingdom was extremely wealthy and who knew what splendours he would endow on the lucky woman he made his Princess. Not to mention a splendid home in Singapore, where he spent a lot of time.

That lucky woman would be married to the most wonderful man, Sally thought. Her envy of his unknown fiancée was not over the riches, but over *him*. He was the prize, not his wealth. She had to shake that thought out of her head. The Edward she'd known could be very different from his princely self.

'Do you know who his fiancée might be?' she asked tentatively.

'Not a clue,' said Iris, who confessed to an avid interest in celebrity gossip. 'His private life is kept private. No scandals that we know of. Which is why we're agog about his engagement. It's like the story of Cinderella—who is the lucky girl whose foot fits the glass slipper?'

'You've got me curious about the Prince,' Sally ventured, proud of how steady she kept her voice. 'You must point him out to me.'

Iris scanned the room. 'Prince Edward is at the VIP table, up front, closest to the stage,' Iris said. 'He's standing up, talking to the chairman of the governing board, I believe. Yes, I can see the chairman, but the Prince has his back to us.'

Sally's heart caught in her throat. *He was here.* Frustratingly, all Sally could see of the man who towered over his companion were his black hair and broad shoulders in a dark tuxedo. She fought the urge to stand up so she could see better. 'I can only see his back,' she said, keeping the frustration from her voice. From this distance he could be any tall man.

'Shame,' said Iris. 'He is extraordinarily good-looking. That's why there's all the fuss. He's also smart and of course so very, very rich.'

'I hope he turns around soon,' Sally said lightly. 'He seems to be wearing a tuxedo. I thought he might be wearing something more elaborate.'

'You mean royal regalia? He might wear traditional clothes in his home country, but when he's here in Singapore he's low-key in the way he presents.'

Low-key. That perfectly described the Edward she had known. Maybe there wasn't such a difference between his two personas.

She was getting increasingly desperate to see his face. And yet she was beginning to get cold feet at the thought of an encounter. Could she really pluck up the courage to approach him—a *prince*—if she got the chance? Would it be wise to do so? She had cherished the memories of that night with him for five long weeks. Yet it appeared he'd been cheating on his soon-to-be fiancée. What kind of man did that make him? A liar and manipulator like Nick Wolfe? Or an arrogant playboy prince used to taking what he wanted and intent on one last fling?

Edward was at the gala dinner with great reluctance. Undoubtedly the cancer research institute was a very worthy cause. His family-owned telco company, which he headed, was responsible for the institute's telecommunications, and he was a generous donor. But not only was the event more than a touch tedious, and the speeches interminable, he knew that there was an undercurrent of interest about his marital status buzzing through the ballroom. He hated being the focus of such attention.

Media speculation on his impending engagement was becoming frenzied. Not that he or his family had given even a hint of any such action to be taken. But a snippet had been leaked from somewhere, perhaps from his prospective fiancée's side. When he found out where it had come from, there would be trouble.

Perhaps the leak had been intended to hasten his proposal. Because he was certainly guilty of delaying, of putting every obstacle he could legitimately find in the way of a commitment.

His father had expressed ill-concealed annoyance. His mother had gently reminded him of his duty—his duty to make a loveless marriage. The more he thought about it, the more his inner despair grew. Yet he had grown up knowing that duty always came before personal desires. His uncles' decadent defiling of the age-old traditions had proved what happened when they were reversed.

He had had another meeting with Princess Mai, and it had gone no better than the first. She was undoubtedly very pretty, but the ten-year age gap between them might as well have been one hundred years for all they had in common. Conversation had been stilted on both sides. Marriage was beginning to look like a life sentence rather than something to anticipate.

Trouble was, he was unable to get out of his mind the night with Sally, the beautiful English stranger. Even a pretty princess could come nowhere near Sally, if indeed that had been her name. He had felt more excitement and emotion in one night with her than he believed he ever would with Mai in a lifetime. No matter how many times he told himself his time with Sally had been a steamy casual encounter, he knew it had been something so much more. He had felt something for her he had never felt before. Something indefinable he wanted to find again—and he knew he wouldn't find it with Mai.

Even with a different choice of bride, he would never feel again what he'd felt for Sally in the brief magical interlude when he had been just Edward, with none of the expectations that came with his royal status. She hadn't known him as a crown prince but as a man. He had been himself with her—and she had come to his bed purely to be with him, not for what she could get from him or to solve a political impasse.

The meal and the speeches over, he signalled to his bodyguards—always a presence when he was in public—that he intended to make an exit before dessert was served. He could have left discreetly via a backstage door. Instead he chose to walk down the centre of the ballroom. While he despised publicity, he knew any mention of him in the media would also mean a mention for the cancer research institute. Besides, there were people in the room he had to acknowledge with a brief greeting or even just a nod.

He was part way down the room when he saw her.

Sally.

He broke step, froze, then quickly recovered himself.

Could it be true?

His heart thudded and his mouth went dry. He looked again.

She was here.

His one-night lover was sitting at one of the tables, her head turned towards him as if, perhaps, someone had pointed him out to her.

He recognised her immediately, even though she looked very different to when he had last seen her. Now she wore a formal dress; then she'd worn nothing at all. Now her hair was swept up off her face; then it had been spread across his pillow and he had fisted it in his hands as he had kissed her. If he'd had any doubt it was Sally, and not someone with a strong resemblance to her, it dissipated at the flash of recognition in her eyes. Recognition and a fleeting glimpse of panic. Something in her expression told him that his anonymous Edward cover had been completely blown.

What was she doing here?

His first impulse was to head straight for her, to exclaim his surprise at her presence, and express his pleasure at seeing her again. But common sense restrained him. The rumours of his impending engagement were rippling through the room. He reminded himself again that anyone with a camera phone was a potential paparazzo. There were a lot of curious eyes on him. He could not be seen singling out this woman any more than on the day he had rescued her from the swimming pool.

But nothing could make him walk past her without stopping.

Thankfully, he recognised the man seated near her as Oscar Yeo, the eminent landscape architect, who had worked with his sister Jennifer on several occasions. What was Sally doing at Yeo's table?

Edward stopped as he reached the table. Oscar and his wife rose to greet him with expressions of surprised pleasure. Sally was sitting next to Yeo's wife. She was even lovelier than he remembered, elegant, sophisticated, regal even. The colour drained from her face as she slowly rose too. He noticed she had to clutch the back of her chair for support. Was she, like him, re-membering that the last time she had seen him she had fallen asleep in his arms, both of them spent from the passion they had shared? Every-thing he'd felt that night came flooding back.

He still wanted her more than any other woman.

It took formidable restraint not to ignore his surroundings and sweep her into his arms. In-stead he had to make sure his eyes didn't stray to Sally instead of the Yeos.

'Mr Yeo,' Edward said. 'My sister was full of praise for the last hotel landscape design you did for her.' He shook the landscape architect's hand.

'Thank you,' Yeo said. 'As always, it was a pleasure to work with Princess Jennifer.'

Edward liked that the older man didn't ap-pear overawed at his royal status. The way Ed-ward saw it, he would like to be Edward Chen when he was living and working in Singapore, the Crown Prince when he was in his own coun-try. Although others didn't see it that way—his royal status was the first thing people recognised him by and judged him on. Only that night with Sally, in the privacy of the hotel room, had he been able to be himself. Secure in his anonymity, he had relaxed. She too had been free from expectations, uninhibited and delightful.

'My wife, Iris,' said Yeo, by way of introduction.

Flustered, Mrs Yeo bobbed a quick curtsy.

Edward allowed himself a slight inclination of his head towards Sally, as was the polite thing to do to another member of Yeo's party. She kept her eyes downcast. He suspected she, like him, was terrified of letting slip any prior knowledge of each other by the merest change in her expression.

'May I introduce Sally Harrington,' said Yeo.

She was real.

Sally was a genuine first name. Now she also had a genuine surname. She hadn't lied to him by inventing a fake identity and that pleased him.

'Edward Chen,' he said. She looked up to him and their eyes met. He saw not just recognition but also a fleeting flash of joy. Royal protocol dictated that he be always the first to offer his hand to shake. She took his hand in a firm businesslike grip, but he was aware of her pulse fluttering. Her touch triggered a flood of sensual memories. But he was careful not to hold her hand for a second longer than politeness dictated.

Too many interested eyes were on him. He could not risk revealing how affected he was by this unexpected reunion.

He doubted there was a woman in the room more beautiful than Sally Harrington in a shimmering gown that hinted at her curves rather than flaunted them. High heels brought her eyes so much closer to his than when she'd been barefoot in that black velvet robe.

Did she remember?

He wanted to ask her that, ask her so much more. He gritted his teeth against his frustration that he couldn't acknowledge her. He wanted to ignore everyone else at the table. Instead he had to continue the charade that they were strangers to each other.

Oscar Yeo continued the introduction. 'Ms Harrington is an important client of mine, here from London.'

Edward found it difficult to school his expression to hide his surprise. Who was she? Not just a tourist in Singapore, it seemed. He fought his inclination to issue a string of commands for her to answer about who she was and why she was here.

'Indeed,' he said instead.

'She is from the Harrington Hotel family and we are working with her on a project through our London office.'

A tightening of her lips let him know she didn't want Yeo to spill any further details of that project. He found that intriguing. Or was she just nervous about encountering him?

'I stayed at the Harrington Park in Regent's Park with my family many years ago,' he said. From his memory, it had been a very grand hotel indeed.

'The Harrington Park is our flagship,' she said without elaborating further.

These days, the royal family stayed only at their family-owned hotels. Under his sister's management the portfolio had expanded considerably. However, when in London they stayed at their apartment in Mayfair. He'd had cause to use it when he was studying at Cambridge and went down to London. He vaguely remembered his sister saying that the Harrington Park had changed hands quite recently. She'd considered making an offer, but it had sold immediately to an unknown buyer for an undisclosed sum. How could that be if it was a family enterprise?

'My sister Jennifer is a hotelier,' he said, deliberately downplaying her role as CEO across a vast portfolio.

'How interesting,' Sally said. He saw the cool, self-possessed businesswoman. But the tension hunching her shoulders betrayed her discomfort. No wonder, as the other women at the table were agog even at this businesslike conversation between them. He was very conscious of eyes that went from him to Sally and back again—not just at this table but what felt like the entire ballroom.

'I believe my sister would be interested in meeting another woman in the same business as her.'

'I would like to meet her too. It does tend to be a male-dominated industry.' She spoke with just the right amount of professional interest and courtesy. How did she really feel about seeing him again? He ached to find out.

'Are you in Singapore for long?'

'I fly out tomorrow afternoon,' she said.

'Perhaps you have a business card I could pass on to my sister?'

'Er...certainly,' she said, with the first break in her composure. She reached down to the table to a small beaded purse in the same colour as her dress, fumbled for a moment and pulled out a very smart business card. Her tension was palpable, not perhaps to the others at the table, but he had spent an evening learning her body.

'Thank you,' he said. He slid her card into his inside jacket pocket without looking at it; that would only cause speculation. He felt a rush of exultation.

He had her phone number.

But he schooled his voice to be businesslike. 'I'm sure you'll hear from Jen, if not while you are in Singapore, the next time she is in London.'

'I'll look forward to that,' Sally said.

He ached to pull her into his arms and rush her with him out of the hotel and somewhere private. But cameras would flash if he did so. He tried to express all that in a glance he held for a second too long for a businesslike exchange. But she did not drop her cool façade and her eyes told him nothing.

As he walked away from the table he was aware of her gaze following him. He felt more alive, more invigorated than he had since he'd awoken to that empty bed five weeks ago.

No matter the risk, he had to see her again.

With an inestimable feeling of loss, Sally watched Edward walk away from the table. Two burly bodyguards followed at a distance. There was still time for her to make her excuses to the Yeos, pick up her skirts and rush after Edward, barrelling her way past the bodyguards. But she would only make an utter fool of herself.

There had been a glimmer of recognition in his eyes, for sure, but that was all. However, as soon as she'd seen his face, all the attraction, the excitement, the intense feelings he'd aroused on that day five weeks ago had come rushing back. She'd wanted to drink in his features, touch him, reassure herself he was very real. Hold him. Kiss him.

The father of her baby.

But his princely status put an unscalable barrier between them. The fact he was about to get engaged made the barrier even higher, put barbed wire and shards of glass on top.

As soon as he was out of sight, she had to field questions from Iris. 'Prince Edward asked for your card! What could that mean?'

Sally had to force herself to smile at the buzz of excitement from Iris and the others at the table. Left to herself, she would weep.

'He wanted my card for his sister, not him,'

she said, trying to sound light-hearted and as if their meeting had no significance.

'I wonder if Princess Jennifer will get in touch,' Iris persisted.

'It would be nice if she did, but I very much doubt it,' Sally said. 'My brother often thinks he's found someone or something that would interest me. I just humour him and never follow it up. The Prince's sister might be the same.'

Did she protest too much? Or not show enough excitement at the honour of having been singled out by a prince? Trouble was, she wanted him as much as she had back in his hotel room all those weeks ago, wanted him so much she ached to be with him. It was an effort to feign indifference.

Coming here had been a hideous mistake. It was so much worse to see him and know she could never again be with him. It would have been better if he had remained in the realm of her dreams and fantasies.

'He's so handsome, don't you think?'

'He most certainly is,' Sally said lightly, while fending off a stab of pain at Iris's words. 'I was so glad to have got a good look at him. Now I see what the fuss is all about. His fiancée is a lucky lady.' Not so lucky that her fiancé had cheated on her. For the first time? For the ump-teenth time? Again, she wondered what kind of a man Edward really was.

'She certainly is,' sighed Iris.

'I suppose you see royals all the time in London,' said one of the other women.

'Not really,' she said. 'Although I don't live far from Kensington Palace so I'm always hoping to catch sight of Prince William or Catherine.'

She'd gone to school with a minor royal but didn't think that was worth mentioning. Nor did she see fit to mention that she was related to a duke way back on her mother's side of the family tree. And that her great-great-great-something grandfather, the founder of the Harrington Park, was the youngest son of an earl. He'd had no chance of inheriting the title and had gone very successfully into commerce. The fact that blue blood—somewhat diluted—ran in her and her brothers' veins wasn't something they had been brought up to trade on. In fact, she wondered if her brothers had even listened to their grand-mother's stories about their titled ancestors. They were Harringtons; that was enough. Jay wouldn't give a toss and Hugo…well, Hugo was a stranger to her now and she had little idea of what was important to him.

'How exciting. London must be a fabulous place to live,' said the same woman.

'I could say the same about Singapore,' Sally said. 'I love it here.'

While she kept on top of the conversation, underneath all she could think about was Edward, the touch of his hand on hers, how incredibly good he looked in a perfectly tailored tuxedo, how he was a *prince* and utterly and totally out of her reach.

She managed to get through the rest of the evening. Back in her hotel room, she stood looking in the mirror, fighting back tears of despair, overwhelmed by an uncharacteristic self-doubt. What had he seen in her? Not enough to be interested, that was for sure. But why should he show interest? The man was about to get engaged.

Sally heaved a great sigh of regret, consigning Edward—*Prince Edward*—to the past. She slipped off her new shoes with some relief. She slid out of her beautiful new dress with a pang; she wouldn't be able to fit into it for much longer.

She started to take off her make-up in the bathroom when her phone pinged a text message.

Singapore was eight hours ahead of London. At this time of night, it was probably her brother Jay. Or even Hugo. Hugo would certainly be interested in the results of her meeting with Oscar. She hadn't had time to contact either of them, being way too busy getting sorted for the gala. She wasn't really in the mood to talk about the winter garden, but she'd better check the text in case it was something important.

The text wasn't from either of her brothers. Rather it was from an unknown number. She opened it anyway.

I have to see you. Edward.

Sally stared at the words on the screen, scarcely able to believe them. Disbelief and excitement made her tremble all over. With hands that shook, she tried to text back, but she fumbled the screen and dropped the phone. Finally, she managed to get her thumbs working enough to text a reply.

Yes.

I will send a car to your hotel.

Now?

Be in the foyer in five minutes.

Nothing would stop her from being in that foyer. Her heart was racing. What did he want with her? To warn her to keep their tryst of five weeks ago secret? Was there even a slight chance he was as filled with anticipation as she was? Heaven knew where he intended taking her. He could drive her up and down Orchard Road for all she cared. She ached with a painful intensity to see him. *Just see him.* She would have to wait to see his reaction to her before she considered anything as bold as telling him she was pregnant.

She touched up the make-up she'd been about to remove. Then slipped into narrow black trousers—which now fitted a little more snugly at the waist—black stilettoes and a sleeveless black silk top, layered and trimmed with silk fringing. She left on her grandmother's diamond earrings and bracelet she'd worn to the dinner.

She was going to meet a prince.

Sally silently cursed the slow elevator. Seconds wasted on stabbing the down button were seconds taken from seeing Edward. It was probably six minutes by the time she got to the foyer.

Was he waiting for her?

The concierge approached her and told her that her car was there. He indicated a man dressed in a chauffeur's uniform. Sally fought a sharp pang of disappointment that Edward hadn't come to meet her himself but dismissed the thought immediately. The driver no doubt had his instructions of where to take her. The speculation about Edward's impending engagement had reached fever-pitch after he'd left the Yeo table at the gala. Under that kind of fierce spotlight, he couldn't be seen with her—or any other woman who wasn't his fiancée. Her excitement dimmed a little—she was, when it came down to it, his scandalous little secret.

CHAPTER FIVE

THE CHAUFFEUR OPENED the back door of a sleek black limousine with dark tinted windows and politely ushered Sally towards it. About to climb inside, she paused momentarily. Trust didn't come easily to her, and she was taking a lot on trust, but in that heartbeat of hesitation she decided she had nothing to fear. Or lose.

Edward.

She sensed his presence before she saw him on the other side of the wide seat. Yet so close she could reach out and touch him, if she dared. She turned to face this man she knew so intimately and yet did not know at all.

Why had he cheated on his soon-to-be fiancée?

'Sally,' he said slowly, his eyes intent on her.

Her heart jolted into an erratic rhythm that stole her breath. Back in her hotel room, in those few minutes between getting his text and heading out of the door, she'd practised over and over in her head what she'd say to him—this man she had been unable to forget, who had made love to her and made her laugh, whose baby she carried. But, faced with the regal presence of Crown Prince Edward of Tianlipin, she felt paralysed by nerves, her words frozen on the tip of her tongue. Was she expected to address him as *Your Highness*?

All she could manage was a croaky and totally inadequate, 'Hi.'

He had taken off his tuxedo jacket and rid himself of his bow tie. In white shirt and black trousers, he seemed more like her Edward, where no formalities were required. *Her* Edward? *Huh.* She had no claim whatsoever on this royal personage. Some poor cheated-on woman did. She kept a careful distance from him, at the same time aching to slide across the seat to be nearer.

Edward acknowledged her single word of greeting with a nod. He seemed tense, his face set in rigid lines. But surely not as nervous as Sally, alone with him in the darkened back seat of the car.

Once the driver was settled behind the wheel, Edward reached out to close the communication panel between driver and passengers. 'That's better,' he said as he turned back to face her.

She noted in his dark eyes a shadow of the same uncertainty that choked her words and made her clutch tight the strap of her handbag. But there was nothing to clarify what she was doing there alone with him on the night he'd been expected to announce his engagement. Or to justify the violent whirlpool of her senses that was shaking her off her balance simply by being near him.

'Thank you for agreeing to meet with me,' he said finally, very formally.

She had a polite response ready but other words overwhelmed it and tumbled out of her mouth. 'You're a prince,' she blurted out. 'A real, honest-to-goodness prince. Of all the things I imagined you might be, I never thought of a prince.'

'From a dynasty dating back many hundreds of years.' He paused. 'And I believe you're "hotel royalty".' He made quote marks with his fingers. Long, elegant fingers that had played her body so intimately. She was glad for the darkened interior of the car to hide her blush.

'A tag invented by the media. Not quite the

same thing as your brand of royalty,' she said, a smile tugging at the corners of her mouth.

'Perhaps not,' he said, with an answering lightening of his features.

'You were quick to research me,' she said.

'As soon as I could look at your business card without causing a media meltdown.' The remembered edge of humour to his voice did much to ease her nerves.

'Online there was a lot more about you than you would have found about me,' she said.

Her grip tightened on her handbag with the hope he hadn't read the rundown of her disastrous break-up with the actor in *Celebrity* magazine. Her Ice Queen moniker had got quite an outing in that article.

'I discovered you're a very successful businesswoman, boss of your own company, Sally Harrington Interiors, with clients all around the world. A winner of prestigious design awards. The *London Evening Post* filled me in on the background of your stepfather's bankruptcy and your older brother's subsequent purchase of the Harrington Park Hotel.'

'All correct,' she said. As far as her business success went, she was proud of what she'd achieved, fired by the determination to succeed on her own terms, to never be reliant on a man the way her mother had been.

'For so long, all I knew was your first name, that you were an interior designer and that you liked gardening.'

'I knew even less about you.' But she knew the important, secret things—the way he used his tongue when he kissed; the warm, salty taste of his skin; his moans when she'd discovered his most sensitive spots; how he was ticklish in the crook of his elbow. A shiver of desire rippled through her at the memory, tightening her nipples, making her press her thighs together.

'When did you discover my identity?' he asked.

'Just this afternoon.'

'Only then?'

'I saw you on television. The programme I was watching in my hotel room segued from a report on the admirable health of the Singapore economy to the current status of Asia's most eligible bachelor. I was surprised to find I recognised him.' Surely that day would go down as the most momentous of her life for unexpected discoveries.

'I'm sorry you had to find out that way. You must have been shocked.'

'*Shocked* is probably too mild a word for it.' She couldn't keep the quiver from her voice.

He paused. 'Were you angry I didn't tell you the truth about who I was the last time we met?'

Sally girded herself to provide the nonchalant answers required by the one-night stand rules.

'No. It was only one night. A game. A fantasy.'

He frowned. 'If you put it like that.'

She added some Ice Queen cool to her words. 'That's what we agreed. One time was all we had to offer. No regrets.'

'Do you regret that night?'

She couldn't help the slow smile that curved her lips at the memories of their lovemaking. 'Not for a moment. It was…you were…extraordinary.'

She couldn't mention the unintended and life-changing result of their time together. Not now. Not yet. Maybe never.

He was a prince.

'And you?'

'I regret it was only the one night,' he said hoarsely. He angled his body so he narrowed the gap on the leather seat between them. 'I haven't been able to stop thinking about you.'

Sally stared at him in disbelief and a bubbling of unexpected joy. 'Me too. Stop thinking about you, I mean.' She would be too embarrassed to admit just how much she had thought about him, even dreamed about him—erotic dreams from which she awoke overwhelmed by an aching sense of frustration and loss.

'I tried to find you. By the time I got back from my business trip to Bangkok, you'd checked out of your hotel and flown back to London.'

'How did you know where I was staying?' She paused. 'Never mind. I guess princes have ways of finding out things ordinary people can't.'

He smiled. 'Simple, everyday detection work, I can assure you. But a good hotel doesn't give out names and personal details of its guests, even to royalty. Yours stuck to the rules.'

'Quite rightly,' she said. 'We would do the same at the Harrington Park.' She didn't know whether to be grateful or cranky at her Singapore hotel for its discretion.

He had tried to find her.

And she, in spite of all her fervent self-lectures that it had been *just one night*, had tried to find him. After four days of sleepless nights and distracted days, she'd called his hotel, only to be told there was no Edward staying in that room. No surprises there. Even less surprising now she knew his family owned the hotel.

Her emotions were flip-flopping all over the place. To know he felt in some way the same about their encounter made her spirits soar, and she allowed herself a flash of crazy, one-night stand rule-breaking hope.

But then reality intruded. 'That night. Back then. I asked you if you were married. You said you weren't. But it appears you were about to get engaged. You cheated on your girlfriend. I would *never* date another woman's man. Let alone… let alone sleep with him. You were not honest with me.'

Edward pushed his hands through his hair and uttered a low groan that sounded a mix of frustration and despair. 'She was not my girlfriend. I was not her man. I did not cheat on her with you.'

She frowned. 'So why—?'

'My situation is impossible. I am about to become engaged to the Princess of a neighbouring kingdom.'

Sally's emotions plummeted to painful depths.

How could she compete with a princess?

'Congratulations. That…that's lovely for you.'

'No, it's not.' He thumped his fist on the car seat in an action that made Sally start. 'I finally agreed to a marriage made purely for political and dynastic reasons. I don't even like my future bride, let alone love her. I've only met her twice.'

'You…you don't love her?'

'No.'

'Then why—?'

'Duty. Obligation. The honour of my country.'

She drew back a little. 'So why am I here, alone with you, when you're about to get engaged?'

Not for a booty call, she thought, the words ugly in her mind. That wasn't going to happen. Not when he was about to get engaged. Not when, seeing him again, she wanted him as much as she had five weeks ago and couldn't bear to have him again and lose him again.

'At the gala it seemed unbelievable you were here in Singapore. Despite the risk, I had to stop at your table. But that wasn't enough. I had to see you alone.'

Sally swallowed hard. 'If you're worried I've told anyone about our time together, don't be. I haven't told a soul that I met you, let alone that I…that we—'

He made a dismissive gesture. 'It's not that. I didn't expect anything less of you than discretion. I still don't or you wouldn't be here. But our last meeting had left so much unsaid. I had to talk with you away from the scrutiny of a ballroom full of onlookers. Find out who the real Sally is—obviously more than the mermaid of my memories.'

'You thought of me as a *mermaid?*'

'That's how you looked under the water—your pale skin, your long hair floating around you. You enchanted me.'

'And you were my…my Sir Galahad. But if I was a mermaid I'd be able to swim properly,' she said. 'I still feel embarrassed about that.'

'No need to be. Pulling you from the pool gave me the opportunity to get close to you, a woman I might never have met otherwise.'

'Because you're having an arranged marriage?' The idea seemed so old-fashioned. But she knew different countries had different customs.

'I am Crown Prince of my country.' Both arrogance and pride underscored his words. 'It is expected of me. Marriage for senior members of the royal family is about more than personal desire.'

'I understand,' she said.

But did she really? In her experience, people chose who they wanted to marry. That the choice was always a good one could be debated—look at her mother choosing to marry a horrible man like Nick Wolfe. That choice had caused a wave of repercussions. The splintering of her family. Loss of livelihoods for Harrington employees. A damaged reputation for the Harrington Park that she and her brothers were now trying to claw back.

'My family is complicated,' Edward said.

'So is mine,' Sally said, rather too wholeheartedly.

'In what way?'

'It would take all night to explain,' she said. 'I'd much rather hear about your family—and why you're going to marry someone you don't even like, let alone love.'

'I'd prefer not talk about it here,' he said.

'Then where?'

'The only place we can talk with any real privacy is my place.'

'You mean your palace?'

He laughed. 'I don't have a palace in Singapore.'

'But you do in your home country?'

'A very splendid palace where I have my own apartment.'

I'd like to see that.

The words hung unspoken between them. They both knew she would never see his palace. He was going to marry a princess.

'So you have an apartment here too? Wait. Do you live in that penthouse where we met?'

He shook his head. 'That was temporary while my Singapore home was being remodelled and refurbished.'

'For your future bride?'

'For myself. The interiors were dated and needed refurbishing more to my taste.'

'Is your home far?'

'Not far. Tanglin. Near the Botanic Gardens. You may have visited the gardens on your last trip.'

One of the most exclusive, desirable places to live in Singapore, so Iris had told her in a general discussion about Singapore real estate. Home to multi-million Singapore dollar 'landed houses', increasingly rare in a city of soaring skyscrapers.

'Do you live alone?' She couldn't—*wouldn't*—go there if she were to be judged and scrutinised.

'My sister also shares the house. We have separate residences under the same roof. I live upstairs; she lives downstairs. We're good friends as well as siblings.'

'Is your sister there now?'

'Jen's in Australia. She's acquired a historic building in the heart of the city of Sydney and is repurposing it into a boutique hotel.'

'Can I mention that project if she calls me? You know, to kickstart the conversation?'

He paused for a beat too long. 'Sure. It's no secret.'

Sally narrowed her eyes. 'Will your sister actually call me? Or—'

'She might do. If and when I pass on your card.'

'You asked for my card so you—?'

'Could get your contact details. It was a ploy.' At last a return of his wonderful smile. 'Did you know I would be at the gala?'

Sally didn't want to admit she had been at the gala purely in the hope of seeing him. 'Oscar invited me. Once I knew you would be there, of course I wanted to see you.'

'Would you have sought me out if I hadn't approached you?'

'Unlikely.'

'Why not?'

'You're a prince. I'm, to all intents, a stranger. I had no idea of what my reception might be. Your bodyguards would probably have stopped any approach from me.'

'My bodyguards do as I instruct them.'

'Which is probably to protect you from over-enthusiastic fans. You have many fans. Entire websites and blogs devoted to you.'

'I know,' he said tersely. 'I choose to ignore them.'

'You're a celebrity.'

'Not on my terms. I'm the member of an ancient royal family fulfilling my duties.'

'Who just happens to be movie-star-handsome.'

He growled his very negative response, which made her laugh.

'Well, you are. But even if you were simply Edward, the businessman I thought you to be, I still would have hesitated to approach you. I've never done anything so impulsive as our one night together. Besides, I liked you as Edward. Prince Edward was an unknown quantity.'

'I'm the same person. Can you see that now?'

'I'm beginning to…' she said slowly. But how sure could she be?

His brow furrowed. 'That night. It wasn't just about the sex for me. Although we were sensational together.'

She caught her breath. 'Yes, we were.' For a long moment he fell silent and she wondered if he was reliving, as she was, those passionate moments they had shared.

'I felt something more,' he said. 'A different level of connection.'

She paused, wanting to be sure she used the right words. 'I'm usually cautious when I meet someone new. But I liked you immediately. As well as fancying you.'

'You were a person I wanted to get to know if—'

'Circumstances were different.' This finishing off of each other's sentences didn't seem out of place. In bed they'd each seemed to know instinctively what the other had wanted.

'Our coming together felt like something inevitable,' he said.

'Inevitable but—'

'Impossible,' he said heavily.

He went to take her hand, but Sally gently released it from his clasp. 'You're right; it's impossible. Utterly impossible.' And her pregnancy took it to an entirely new level of impossibility. 'We can talk but we really mustn't touch.'

No touching.

Edward knew she was right. But he was having immense trouble keeping his thoughts on an even keel. In terms of royal protocol—especially at this time of his impending engagement—his impulsive decision to ask Sally to join him at his house would not be seen as wise or advisable. Even more so than before, she was a scandal in the making. But he would regret it for the rest of his life if he had passed on the chance to see her again.

If he were indeed Mr Edward Chen he would have a lot more to say to her about how he'd felt that night five weeks ago, how important and special he'd believed she could have become to him. But he was heir to the throne of the country he loved, who honoured and respected his parents, and a future crown weighed heavily on his head. As Prince Edward he had no choice but to keep her at arm's length.

Common sense dictated he tell the driver to turn around and return his guest to her hotel. But he made no such order. Sally was *real*, more beautiful even than he had remembered. He had slipped so easily back into conversation with her. And he wanted her.

He could not deny himself further time with Sally, stealing every possible second before he had to say goodbye to her—this time for ever.

CHAPTER SIX

SALLY FOLLOWED EDWARD into his house via a dimly lit back entrance to avoid, he said, any possible unwanted media attention. She was aware of palm trees and shrubs and the heady scents of a warm, humid tropical night. Once inside, they shot up in an elevator to his quarters and inside to a blast of air conditioning. It was the upper half of an elegant converted colonial mansion and retained mansion-like proportions as, no doubt, did his sister's floor below.

Edward told her there was separate staff accommodation and he had dismissed the staff for the night, so their privacy was assured. 'You'll have to manage with me looking after you,' he said with a grin.

Sally suppressed a shiver of desire at the thought of the exciting ways he could look after her but forced them to the back of her mind. She'd meant what she said about no touching.

It was the only way she knew to keep her equilibrium.

Pregnant by a prince.

Although that didn't stop her from aching to pull him down with her to one of the oriental day beds in the loggia that seemed placed for their sensual comfort.

'Can a prince operate without staff?' she asked, confident enough now in his company to risk a little teasing. 'The Harrington Park's lore includes tales of a royal personage who demanded staff dip his teabag in his cup for him because he didn't know how.' Sally always wondered why a porcelain teapot wouldn't have been in service for such an esteemed guest but didn't want to ruin the story.

Edward laughed.

She loved his laughter.

'I studied in both the UK and the US. I had bodyguards but their duties didn't include waiting on me. I enjoyed being independent when I got the chance. You can trust me to get you a drink or something to eat.'

Sally realised the risk he took in bringing her alone to his house amid the media frenzy focused on his personal life and she appreciated it.

She would have been heartbroken if he'd dropped her back at her hotel. These bonus moments with him were to be cherished. They were all she would have with him before she flew back to London the next day. Memories stored up from this night and hugged close would have to last a long, long time.

He ushered her through to the living area. She didn't have to feign enthusiasm for his Singapore home. Usually Sally examined interior design with a silent conviction she could do better. In this case she wasn't sure she could. His house was superbly designed and decorated, with dark floors and white walls, contemporary furniture and antique dark carved pieces set off by a perfectly placed collection of Asian and western artworks. She particularly liked the ceramics, which Edward told her were a speciality of Tianlipin.

'My Chinese ancestors brought the skills with them when, many centuries ago, they invaded and conquered the indigenous people living on the island. They had their own skills in wood carving, which became part of our cultural heritage.'

Sally admired an outsize jar that seemed a

museum piece yet sat unprotected on its own pedestal.

Not a house for children.

The thought flashed from nowhere. When she told Edward about her pregnancy it would be his choice if he wanted to have anything to do with the baby's London upbringing. She certainly wouldn't expect or demand it.

'Your ancestors were fierce invaders,' she said.

'Fierce defenders too. Our island has never again been invaded or colonised and our people from different ethnic backgrounds live harmoniously.'

'No uprisings?'

His black brows rose. Again, Sally reminded herself that different places had different cultures and customs. 'I'm not being critical. Remember I live under a monarchy myself.'

'The British monarchy is not quite the same as ours,' he said very seriously. 'We have an elected advisory council, but we are not a democracy. However, my father's rule is, thankfully, a benevolent one.'

'The rulers weren't always benevolent?' Sally was interested in his home country, not so much the politics of it but to extend her knowledge of both him and the heritage of her baby. It was also a relief to talk about something other than their one night together. And to delay the time when she had to confess that she was pregnant. She wanted to enjoy Edward's company a while longer before she faced his reaction to her news. Truth be told, she was still coming to terms with it herself.

Edward heaved a sigh. 'That's where I told you my family was complicated. Let me get drinks and I'll explain.'

He led her to an elegant sofa with dark carved wooden arms, upholstered in cream silk and adorned with vibrantly coloured silk cushions. It was a very fine piece indeed. An identical sofa sat opposite, separated by a marble coffee table.

'White wine?' he asked.

Sally shook her head, searching for an excuse. 'Mineral water with a slice of lemon, please. I've had enough to drink tonight.' He didn't question her choice, although she could tell he was surprised after her enjoyment of the same drink on their first meeting. In fact, she hadn't touched alcohol at all at the gala. Or eaten much food. It was only the excitement of being with Edward that was staving off exhaustion and an underlying nausea that came and went.

'A snack?'

'No, thank you.' Her stomach roiled at the thought. She was too wary to tempt fate by eating.

Edward returned with drinks, whisky for him and her mineral water in a tall frosted glass. He took his place across from her on the opposite sofa with athletic grace. He looked so at home, so unbelievably handsome. She couldn't help but speculate that her child would be good-looking with such a man as their father.

'I noticed in my research into you that you're a twin,' he said.

'Yes, my brother Jay is my twin, the older by just a few minutes.'

Edward held his whisky glass and swirled its contents around without drinking from it. 'Traditionally, in my country, twins are considered to be bad luck and bearers of ill fortune.'

Sally stared at him and felt the colour leach from her face. 'Why would you tell me that when you know I'm a twin?'

'Because, awful as it is, it directly relates to

the story of my family. I don't believe such ignorant superstition, of course. Not for a moment.'

'I should hope not,' she said, affronted. Whether by accident or design, she was grateful for the distance the coffee table put between her and Edward on their opposing sofas.

'Being a twin has only ever been good for me. When you're a twin you're never alone. Jay is my closest friend.' Or he had been until, halfway through the sixth form, he'd upped and left school to work in a restaurant kitchen in Paris. Finishing that last year at St Mary's without him had been difficult. Jay's popularity had shielded his quieter, more aloof sister and she'd been left vulnerable. Sally wasn't sure their close relationship had ever quite recovered from his departure, or whether twins by nature grew apart as they grew up.

'I didn't mean to offend you. I'm sharing this story to help you understand why duty and honour are so important to my family and my country,' he said. 'We have a scandal-ridden past to overcome.'

Sally leaned towards him. 'Sounds intriguing.' The internet had hinted at some old scandal but all she'd been interested in reading about was him, not his ancestors.

'My father was the youngest of three brothers; the oldest were identical twins. They were born five minutes each side of midnight, so the firstborn was theoretically a day older than his twin. My grandfather, then the King, died relatively young when his car went off the road in the mountains. There were suspicions that it hadn't been an accident. Nothing was ever proven, although persistent rumours circulated that his heir, the older twin, burdened by gambling debts the King had refused to cover, had hastened his father's demise to accelerate his accession to the throne.'

Sally's eyes widened. 'That's quite a story.'

'It gets worse. I was only a baby when this all happened, but my father made sure I knew the history so as to understand how it affected us as a family.'

'I can relate to the family history thing,' Sally said. She recalled her mother trying to keep memories of her father and the glory days of the Harrington Park alive for her children. Although never in the presence of Nick Wolfe. Weren't she and her brothers, by the restoration of the hotel, trying to bring back those good times to some-how heal the wounds the loss of their family unit had brought all three?

Edward continued. 'The country was in mourning for their loved and respected King, but his son demanded an inappropriately lavish coronation. He started his reign the way he meant to continue, by draining the country's coffers. He and his twin funded an extraordinarily decadent lifestyle of astonishing excesses. The world's most expensive yachts, cars, jets, racehorses—every overpriced plaything you can think of—this corrupt ruler grabbed in multiples. Women too, to the extent he kept a modern-day harem, some of whom later claimed to have been kidnapped. He and his twin spent large parts of the year in Europe with their international so-called friends, who sponged ruthlessly off them.'

'When did the King find time to rule the country?'

'In our ancient tradition, the King was a man of virtue who appointed other men of virtue as magisterial officers to help him govern.'

'Your uncle turned this on its head?'

'His officials were as corrupt as he was. Taxes were raised to burdensome levels. Bribery became endemic. And still more money left the country to fund the twins' dissolute lifestyles.'

'Sounds the perfect set-up for a revolution,' she said slowly.

'Dangerously so, my father tells me.'

'So what happened?'

'Fate intervened. My uncle, the King of our proud country, died in compromising circumstances in a brothel.'

Sally gasped. 'Murdered?'

'An undiagnosed heart condition accelerated by a cocktail of recreational drugs.'

'So the other twin took over?'

'The weaker twin didn't dare come home without the protection of his brother. He abdicated, put himself into voluntary exile and died not long after. Neither brother had ever married.'

'So they left no heirs?'

'My father, the third son, became King.'

'I don't know a lot about dynasties, but I guess a third son—'

'Hadn't been prepared for it from birth like his brothers had. My father was a scholar—somewhat of a nerd in fact—happy to live his life on the sidelines of the court. But, when duty called, he jumped right in and did his best to repair the damage his brother had done to his beloved country.' Edward's obvious respect for his father shone through his words.

'And you?'

'At the age of ten I became Crown Prince.'

'Your life must have changed.'

'Completely. That's why I'm telling you all this. Duty and honour became all-important. From the time I was ten years old my destiny was drummed into me. It took some years for my father to turn both the finances and the reputation of the royal family around. He did that by reinstating traditional values and a strong moral code of behaviour, but within a modern context.'

'An admirable man, your father.'

'My mother, also. She worked alongside him to regain the respect and love of our people, although she'd never wanted the attention the role of Queen brought with it.'

'Your family history sounds like the plot of a movie. It's a lot to take in.' These people were her baby's ancestors, she reminded herself. Both the good and the bad. As there was in any family.

Edward took a slug of whisky. 'After the precedent set by my corrupt uncles, avoiding scandal became a priority. Their behaviour put the international spotlight on our country and not in a good way. My father has spent more than twenty years trying to subdue it.'

The intensity of his expression tore at Sally's heart. Who knew he had the weight of all this responsibility on his shoulders? 'So now there's that movie-star-handsome Crown Prince doing his best to avoid scandal.'

'Scandal of the rescuing of mermaids kind,' he said wryly.

Sally laughed. But there was an edge to her laughter. Every word he spoke distanced him further and further from her.

'Not that you and I did anything wrong back then,' he said. 'Not that we're doing anything wrong by being alone together now.'

'But not when you're about to get engaged.'

'Correct.' He sighed, loud and heartfelt. 'Then it becomes a betrayal of my father's moral code.'

'But not yours. If you feel so unhappy about your engagement, why go through with it?'

'My uncles did more damage to the country than merely raiding the treasury. They also alienated long-time allies. Our nearest neighbour has, for political reasons of its own, delayed a full resumption of relations with us. Diplomatic and trade efforts can only go so far. A marriage uniting the royal families could do much to cement new bonds.'

Sally had to swallow hard against a sudden lump of hopelessness. 'That's where your Princess is from?'

'Yes.'

Sally could not help but be gratified to see he showed none of the anticipation one would expect of a man in love with a princess.

'Is she crazy about you?'

'She's twenty-one. I'm thirty-one.'

'When I was twenty-one I would have thought you were from a different generation.'

He grimaced. 'Let's just say I don't think she belongs to one of my fan clubs.'

Sally frowned. 'Are you telling me she's reluctantly doing her duty too?' How could any woman not leap at the chance to have him in her bed?

'I would suggest so. We've met twice and it was awkward.'

Sally took a deep steadying breath. How she hated the pretence of this cool conversation about a woman this man, the father of her baby, was going to marry. Marry after having met her just twice. It hurt. Not that she wanted to marry him—even if it had been possible. For all their talk of feeling a special kind of emotional connection, they hardly knew each other. Marriage was something to be slowly weighed and deliberated and never undertaken on impulse. Look at the ongoing damage her mother's ill-considered marriage had brought to her family.

But, ever since Edward had approached her at the gala, the truth had been slowly percolating through the turbulence of her thoughts.

She could so easily fall in love with him.

Prince Edward of Tianlipin was the only man she'd met, since her gay high school friend, who made her spirit truly sing. Her habit of falling for unattainable men had reached its apex.

A persistent inner voice reminded her that this mad spark of attraction had been ignited before she knew he was royalty. But what difference could that possibly make?

'Is she…is she pretty?' Sally hated herself for asking the question, but she couldn't seem to help it.

'Yes. She's pretty,' he said.

His words felt like tiny but deadly stabs from a poisoned stiletto. 'Oh,' she managed to choke out.

Edward got up and in a few steps was beside Sally on her sofa. He looked deep into her eyes. 'But nowhere near as beautiful as you.' He reached out to cradle her face in his hands, warm and strong and possessive. 'There is no woman more beautiful than you, Sally Harrington.'

As she breathed in his scent, lemongrass and sandalwood—already heart-stoppingly familiar—she had to momentarily close her eyes at the ecstasy of his closeness. She reached up to place her hands over his. Her *no touching* embargo crumbled.

'That's very kind of you to say but—'

'Please. No self-deprecating remark of the kind you English are so good at. Even half drowned, your face pale with panic, you were beautiful. In a hotel dressing gown you were beautiful. When I saw you at the gala tonight you took my breath away. All you needed was a tiara to look more of a princess than a princess born to it.' His voice was thick with emotion.

Sally turned her head away from him, caught her breath on a barely suppressed sob. 'Please don't talk like that when we both know there's no future possible for us.' A *future* for them? How had she let herself voice the word? There could perhaps be some contact for their child if Edward wanted it, but not for her.

She knew now was the time to tell him about the baby, but she couldn't bear to ruin the moment. She had no idea how he would react, but a pregnancy wasn't the news he'd be welcoming from a one-night stand, even if he wasn't a prince.

'I know very well I shouldn't be saying it but it's difficult not to,' he said. 'Nobody and nothing have ever made me feel the way you do.'

'Same…same for me,' she managed to choke out.

She sat very still as he traced her features with his fingers as if learning her face, as if *memorising* her for a time he would no longer see her. He continued to lightly stroke down her cheekbones, her nose and then feather across her lips in the most subtle of caresses.

Her body felt hyper-sensitive to his touch, delight and arousal thrumming through every nerve-ending. She was tired, emotional, surging with pregnancy hormones. But her overriding feeling was an overwhelming need to be close to him All reason, all common sense was pushed away. She wanted him so badly she ached.

For just one more night.

Her lips parted as invitation to his kiss and she held her breath until he took it. His mouth was tender, undemanding and as she kissed him back she felt the rest of the world fade away until he became her world.

Edward.

He pulled back from the kiss and looked deep into her eyes. Words became superfluous as they exchanged unspoken messages. Assent was asked, consent given. When his mouth came down on hers, passionate and demanding, she responded with a heartfelt whimper of need as she pressed her body close to his. The rights and wrongs of them being together, the *impossibility* of it, were subsumed in a rush of heat and desire.

Edward had never wanted a woman as much as he wanted this one.

Sally Harrington.

Now he had a name for her and a place for her in the wider world. But she had occupied a prominent place in his thoughts for the past five weeks. He could scarcely believe she was now again in his arms. Lovely, sexy, smart Sally. Sally who'd listened so sensitively to the story of his family's recent ugly past. Who had shown nothing but non-judgmental support for him. And who, sensual and responsive, seemed to want him as much as he wanted her.

It felt so right to have her in his house—but wrong to have to hide her away. He wanted more time with her—proudly and out in the open. And yet that decision wasn't his to make. He had no right to date her. Once he became engaged he would become a pawn in a game of politics. Sally would fly back to England the next day to resume her life independently of him.

For the first time, he truly resented the crown's control over his life.

He did not want to marry Princess Mai.

At the age of ten he had been tipped out of a more normal life—or as normal as any members of the royal family were able to live—and thrust into the role of Crown Prince. In the pressure cooker atmosphere of a new royal family intent on righting festering wrongs in as short a time period as possible, he had been forced to grow up quickly. Because he was intelligent, personable and tall for his age, he had become rather more involved in the ins and outs of his father's new role than perhaps had been appropriate for a young boy. He'd seen the harm caused by his uncles' misdemeanours, been horrified by things he hadn't really understood at the time. He'd readily taken on board his father's edict of putting honour and duty above all—after all, his father was now also his ruler.

There'd been some teenage rebellion, but very minor. He genuinely hadn't wanted to disappoint his parents. In his sophomore year at university in Singapore he'd fallen in love. Lim Shu had been clever, vivacious and sweet. She had been deemed unsuitable in that she'd been of low birth and social status. Her family had been paid off and Lim Shu had disappeared from campus without him even getting to say goodbye. He'd been gutted—but eventually resigned to a future that had been predetermined for him. When doing postgraduate study at Harvard he'd met another serious contender for his heart. That time he'd ended it before the blossoming relationship could result in heartache for both of them. He hadn't told his father but had later discovered the King had put eyes on his girlfriend from their first date. He continued to date but was careful to guard his heart.

In spite of all this, Edward had never been

roused to seriously fight against the many things forbidden to him. He hadn't wanted something enough to battle for it.

Until now. Her. Sally.

He could not imagine anything he wanted more than to be with this woman, and not just for another stolen night.

She could be important to him.

They needed time together to get to know each other. But tonight was all he had been granted. He would have to do something about that.

Sally's kisses were fierce and demanding in response to his possession of her lovely mouth. She opened up to him and moaned a sweet sound of deep need as she snuggled closer to him on the sofa. Man, she was hot in subtle, sexy black, the trousers hugging the curves of her hips and those long, long legs. Since she'd got in the car, the layers of fringing on her top had driven him crazy—the way they accentuated the swell of her breasts.

At last he slid his hands under her top and cupped her breasts in his hands. He loved her murmurs of pleasure as he pushed the lacy top of her bra aside and played with her nipples to bring them to tight peaks.

Her pleasure gave him pleasure.

Was his memory playing tricks on him, but did her breasts feel fuller than when he'd last had the pleasure of caressing them?

His hands slid to her waist as he lowered her to the sofa. She squirmed with anticipation as he ran his fingers around the waist of her trousers, looking for the fastening. In turn, she tugged his shirt free of his trousers, grappled impatiently with studs and buttons so she could slide her hands across his back and chest, on a path of exploration and discovering. He took a sharp, deep intake of breath at the intensity of pleasure when she headed with unerring accuracy to his most sensitive spots. Not the least of his delight was that she had remembered what pleased him most.

It took a huge effort of will for him to put a halt to such intoxicating exploration. He didn't want to waste even a minute of his precious time with her. But since the media interest in his engagement had intensified he had become even more protective of his privacy.

He hugged Sally tight and then pulled back to break the kiss, well aware they were about to spontaneously make love on his sofa. Sally murmured her protest, her eyes dazed and unfocused. Her mouth was pouting and swollen from his kisses, her hair falling loose from the knot at her neck. He reached out and undid the pins so her hair tumbled down her shoulders, gloriously glossy and untamed. Had a more magnificent woman ever been born?

'Those large windows are at the front of the house,' he said. 'There are gardens and high walls between us and the street. But the media can be cunning. Who knows where they could gain access with their lenses?'

Her lips pursed into a tiny moue of displeasure which he found very cute. 'So you're saying we should stop? Because I don't want to stop. Not for a moment do I want to—'

'Hell, no. I'm saying I take you to the bedroom, which has blackout curtains and total privacy. There we can be as uninhibited as we want.'

She smiled, a slow seductive smile that sent his blood racing. 'Is that a promise?'

'You can count on it,' he said hoarsely, transfixed by that smile.

'Better get on with it then,' she said, stretching her arms above her head indolently, sensually, her top rucked up to reveal the underside of her breasts, her trouser zip half undone.

Edward needed no further invitation. He stood up from the sofa, reluctant to let go of her in case she disappeared, a fantasy woman he'd conjured up from the intensity of his longing for her. He leaned down and effortlessly swept her into his arms. She felt very, very real.

'Just like last time,' she murmured as she looped her arms around his neck. 'This is getting to be a habit—one I like a lot.'

Once in the seclusion of his bedroom, despite his high level of excitement, he forced himself to take his time, to tease her with a slow stripping of her clothes, a sensual exploration of her body, to take her to the peaks, prolong her pleasure, watch her face as she came. But she was too impatient for him to enter her so they could come together. Who was he to argue? After all, they had hours left to experiment with further ways to please each other.

When they were finally both sated, he lay on his back with her head resting on his chest, her glorious hair spilling across him. The ceiling fan flicked languorously overhead as he drifted into drowsiness. He noticed a tiny translucent gecko resting high on the wall and wondered if Sally was the type to freak out over such realities of living in the tropics. Life both in Singapore and in Tianlipin was very different to life in London.

He knew he should wake her and take her back to the hotel, but he simply couldn't bring himself to do it. Rather, he shifted a little to readjust her weight on his shoulder.

She stirred. 'There's something I really have to tell you,' she murmured, barely audible, without opening her eyes.

'It can wait until later,' he whispered as he drifted into sleep.

CHAPTER SEVEN

SALLY AWOKE IN Edward's bedroom, the early morning sun filtering through the blinds. She was disappointed to find she was alone in the enormous bed. Where was he? For a moment she luxuriated in the pale linen sheets, stretching, recalling the ecstasy of their lovemaking of the night before. Was there time for another—?

With the soft chiming of a clock from somewhere in the house, reality hit.

What was she doing still here?

She sat up abruptly. Edward had agreed that it wouldn't be wise for her to stay. But neither of them had been able to say goodbye and they'd fallen asleep in each other's arms.

On a surge of panic, she checked her watch. Her flight home was scheduled for two p.m. She had to get back to her hotel, pack and be at Changi Airport in plenty of time for her international flight back to London. The taxi to the airport had been booked well in advance. She liked to leave as little as possible to chance. Chance had never served her well. But she still had time. There wasn't much to pack. The ride to the airport only took twenty minutes.

She wouldn't have missed her *just one night more* with Edward for anything. But she was running out of time to tell him she was pregnant. It might be better to do it this way. If things got awkward there would be little time for recriminations.

The uncomfortable stirrings of nausea made her lie back against the pillows and take deep breaths to try and fight it. There were dry crackers in her handbag but where was it? In Edward's living room. Where was Edward? Where, in fact, was the living room? She could remember being carried from the living room by that gorgeous man in a fever of urgency and arousal, but that wasn't useful for directions. This could get awkward.

She was preparing to slide out of bed and retrieve some clothes from where they'd been tossed randomly around the room when Edward came in. He wore white boxers, a smile, and carried a large bamboo tray. Her heart seemed to miss a beat. He was, quite simply, the most wonderful man she'd ever known. Even in the midst of her battle against nausea she took a moment to appreciate her lover's splendid body. He was an athlete in bed, but she knew so little about him she didn't even know what sports he played to achieve his honed athletic shape. The thought made her immeasurably sad. How likely was it that she would ever know?

She pulled the linen sheet up over her breasts, false modesty, she knew, when they had bared everything to each other the night before. But that had been in the heat of passion. This was the reality of the morning after for lovers who scarcely knew each other. However, last night she thought she had known everything she needed to know about Edward.

How could she bear to say goodbye?

'You've made breakfast?' she asked in amused disbelief.

'I dismissed the staff, if you remember. We still have the house to ourselves.'

'Being served breakfast by a prince—now that's a first,' she said.

Even the word 'breakfast' made her feel nauseous. She tried to force anticipation and appetite into her voice. But, as he came closer, so did the smells from the tray and its bounty of tropical fruits.

'Fresh fruit to start,' he said.

He indicated slices of pineapple; starfruit; mango cut into cubes; dragon fruit with its seed-flecked white flesh and hot pink skin; purple passionfruit sliced in half to reveal golden flesh and dark seeds; tiny plump bananas in blemish-free yellow skins. Oh, for such bounty in a cold, grey London winter. On her travels she always took the opportunity to savour exotic fruits. But there was papaya on the tray too, and she'd never liked the smell of that particular tropical fruit. It rose up into her nostrils and made her gag.

'S-sorry.' Sally clamped her hand over her mouth against the overwhelming wave of nausea and leapt out of the bed. She made it to his en suite bathroom just in time, slamming the door shut behind her. The episode was more dry retching than anything, but it left her shaken and weak. She leaned against the cool tiles of the bathroom wall and wished herself anywhere but here. Her body had betrayed her.

She splashed her face with cold water, cleaned her teeth with one of the spare toothbrushes, finger-combed her hair back from her face.

When she knew she couldn't stay hiding in there any longer, she wrapped an enormous white bath towel around her, tucking it firmly between her breasts.

On shaky legs, she emerged from the bathroom. Edward had thrown on a wheat-coloured linen robe over his boxers. He stood by the bed, the breakfast tray abandoned on a nearby table. His expression was inscrutable. 'Are you okay?' he asked.

Wordlessly, she nodded.

'Food poisoning?'

She shook her head, summoning the courage to tell him the truth. 'I… I'm pregnant.'

'By me?'

'Yes.'

'When were you going to tell me?'

'I only found out myself yesterday. It…it came from out of the blue.'

'Are you sure?'

'Sure that I'm pregnant or that you're the father?'

His expression didn't change. 'That you're pregnant.'

'I did three different tests from the pharmacy yesterday. All showed a definitive yes. And there are…symptoms.' He started to say something, but she cut across him. 'There has been no other man in my life for a long time. There can be no doubt you're the father.'

'I would not have doubted your word.'

'And another thing. I thought I was protected. After all, I was on the pill. But I travel so frequently across time zones I might have missed one or taken it at the wrong time. It…it was careless of me.'

'The responsibility wasn't all yours,' he said. 'I should also have taken precautions.'

'That night. I'm usually a dot the Is and cross the Ts person, but… I wanted you so much I… didn't think any further than being with you.' She put up her hand in a halt sign. 'Before you say anything further, I want this baby. Very much so. But I don't intend to make any demands on you. I can support him or her perfectly well on my own and—'

He reached out and gripped the top of her arms. 'Stop. Please. I need time to think. This… this changes everything between us.'

Sally realised she hadn't let Edward get much of a word in. She felt mortified. To have joyful, uninhibited sex on a one-night stand and then be confronted with news of pregnancy would be more than a shock.

It had been a shock for her too. She sat down on the edge of the bed, feeling drained and empty. Unable to say another word, she watched as he paced the length of the bedroom.

Finally, he turned to face her. His face was creased with concern, not anger. 'If I was simply Mr Edward Chen, I would ask you to marry me straight away.'

Sally's hand went to her heart and she stared at him, unable to find the right words to reply. Hot, handsome and *honourable*. For a moment she really wished he was just Mr Chen and that she was the marrying kind.

'That's so lovely of you to say so.' She wanted to get up and give him a hug but she was feeling too shaky to do so. Instead, she reached up and clasped his hand.

'I mean it,' he said.

He squeezed her hand, then sat down next to her on the edge of the bed as he released it. She was sitting next to a prince and she was wearing only a towel. Not that he was clad in much more: a pair of boxers and a robe tied so loosely that it fell open from the waist so she could admire his smooth, muscular chest. The bed, with rumpled sheets and clothing tossed every which way, was testament to the enjoyment they had given each other.

'I actually believe you do.' She smiled a wobbly, poor excuse for a smile. 'But…*marriage*.'

He frowned. 'You say it as if it were something not under any consideration.'

'Even if you were free to marry, it wouldn't be on the cards.'

'What do you mean?'

'We barely know each other. Our lives are on opposite sides of the world.'

'Neither is an insurmountable problem.'

'We're still speaking hypothetically, right?'

'For now.' She noted the stubborn set of his jaw. A future ruler in training for when his word became law. How little she knew about him. But she was beginning to realise he could be formidable.

'How could it ever be any different for us?'

'There could be options.'

She raised her eyebrows. 'Even so, accidentally getting pregnant isn't reason enough to marry a stranger.'

Edward didn't seem like a stranger to her—

hadn't from the first—and from the ill-disguised anguish on his face she didn't think she felt like a stranger to him either. But she had to face facts. The Ice Queen hadn't got where she was by dealing in fantasies.

'Perhaps so,' he said. 'However, I come from a family—a culture—that reveres our ancestors. Your baby—*our* baby—carries the blood of a dynasty dating back many hundreds of years. He or she will be part of that unbroken line.'

Sally froze, stymied by this new information. She hadn't been pregnant long enough, or had enough knowledge of her baby's father, to even think about the immensity of such connections. What had she got herself into, albeit inadvertently?

'But on the wrong side of the blanket, as they say.'

'Which is why any possibility of marriage must be explored. The rules are strict in the Tianlipin royal family. Only legitimate offspring can be in line to the throne.'

Her baby could be in line to an ancient Asian throne? It was almost too much to take in.

'I didn't realise all the ramifications of you

being royal.' She couldn't help the note of rising panic in her voice.

'How could you have, when you've only just learned my identity?'

It felt surreal to be having a conversation like this. Although she suspected the only way it could end would be with her signing legal letters from his family relinquishing any claims on him in return for a hush-hush pay-out. She would, of course, refuse any money.

'I would never make any claim on you or…or your throne.'

'No matter what, the child will be blood of my blood.' It seemed an old-fashioned term but she got exactly what he meant—and didn't miss the note of fierce possession in his voice.

She still felt too shaky to get up from the bed, but she sat up straighter to face him. 'Yesterday, when I discovered I was pregnant, all I knew of you was the name *Edward*. It might have been a false name, for all I was aware. The pregnancy blindsided me. I stared at three positive pregnancy kits over and over, shook them, waved them about, while they continued to give the same result. But I decided I would be the best sole parent I could possibly be. I'm more than capable of giving this baby a good life. I don't need you.'

Edward took a quick intake of breath at her bluntness. 'But the baby might.'

His reply seemed to hit her with equal impact. 'Yes,' she said slowly. 'A child has a right to know their father.'

'And a father to know his child.'

Sitting near him on the edge of the bed, she looked listless and as pale as the white towel tucked somewhat precariously between her breasts. Of course her breasts had felt larger. Because she was pregnant. And having a tough time of it already. He was still reeling from the impact of her news.

He was going to be a father.

'My child will grow up with me in London,' she said. 'You could play a role in their life. If not as their acknowledged father, as a…a trusted family friend or—'

Edward gave a snort somewhere between laughter and disbelief. 'One thing that will become immediately apparent after the birth is that your child's father is Asian. I might not be so easy to sweep under the carpet. There'd be questions asked about a friend who flies in from Singapore for visits.'

Sally smiled. 'If our child takes after you, he or she is sure to be beautiful. I didn't plan to get pregnant but…but I chose my baby's father well.'

'Thank you. I can say the same about you, lovely Sally.' He put his arm around her shoulders and drew her close. She snuggled against him, warm and trusting in spite of her uncertainty of what faced her. He wanted to shield and protect her. But there could be battles ahead.

'We don't find ourselves in an easy situation, do we?' he said.

'That's one way of putting it,' she said.

'Somehow I'll find a way to make it work.'

'Like royal families have been doing for ever, I should imagine,' she said. 'In the old days of our monarchy, a pregnant mistress would be married off to someone willing to give the child a name and sent off to live in the country.'

'You're not marrying anyone,' he growled in a sudden surge of possessiveness. 'And you're not my mistress. If you were, the solution would be simple. I could revive the old custom of appointing an official mistress or consort.'

She broke away from his embrace. '*What?* Are you serious?'

'In the old days of our monarchy it was common. But, to my knowledge, there hasn't been an official mistress since the nineteen-twenties.'

'Marry the Princess and have me as a mistress? You must be joking.'

'Of course I am.' He only wanted one wife. A wife to love and cherish. Besides, the King and Queen would forbid it. He almost laughed out loud at the thought of presenting the idea to his strait-laced father.

'Good,' she said. 'I don't need to be married or anyone's mistress—official or otherwise. I can handle having the baby on my own.'

Before he had a chance to reply, his cell phone rang from where it sat on the side table. He let it ring out, but it rang again, and then again. 'I'd better answer,' he said, annoyed by the interruption. He got up. 'My sister,' he said when her ID flashed up. 'She's due back from Sydney this morning.'

He took the call, listened intently and ended it

with a string of curses. He turned to Sally, gritted his teeth. 'The media have got scent of you.'

'Of *me*?'

'Of a mystery woman driven here last night.'

It was Sally's turn to utter a few choice words. 'I can't have them find out who I am. Or, heaven forbid, that I'm pregnant.'

'You don't look—'

'When I bought my dress for the gala, the sales assistant knew I was pregnant immediately. I'd only just discovered it myself. Others might have the same skill.'

'Needless to say, I don't want it known either.'

Sally cautiously got up from the bed. The towel slipped open momentarily. She really didn't look pregnant to him; perhaps at this stage only a woman in the know would twig to her condition. 'You don't want the media attention but neither do I,' she said. 'My brothers and I are relaunching the Harrington Park and the last thing we need is me getting caught up in a scandal. We're trying to restore the reputation my stepfather trashed. I don't want to give people anything else to gossip about.'

She closed her eyes tight, as if against the very thought. He realised they had spoken about his complicated family, but he knew very little about hers. Her voice hitched. 'They'll rehash my love life too.'

He had tortured himself with thoughts of her with another man. 'What do you mean?'

'I was in a relationship with a quite well-known actor and it ended badly. The press had a field day. It was more than a year ago. But I can't have them speculating I've set my sights on a soon-to-be-married prince. And it wouldn't end at that. When my baby is born, they'll count back to my time in Singapore.'

'According to my sister, they believe the woman is my mystery fiancée. They're determined to track down her identity. As I'd feared, a contingent of reporters and photographers have set up outside.'

'This is a disaster.' Sally snatched her hand to her mouth. 'How will I get out of here? I have to go back to the hotel, pack, then get out to the airport.'

'You can't. They'll follow you to the hotel. By now they might have traced my car back to the hotel. It will only take someone to identify you from the gala last night—'

'And I'm in trouble.'

'*We're* in trouble.'

'You might be in even worse trouble than I would be. Not just from your family but from your Princess's family.'

'That would be a real storm of a scandal.'

'I'm sorry,' she said.

'Why be sorry? I don't regret anything between us, do you?'

'Not at all,' she said.

'But it would be better to keep the media out of it.'

'What do we do?' He noticed the green tinge to her skin and hoped she wasn't going to be ill again.

'Take you somewhere the press can't follow.'

She gestured with her hands to encompass the world. 'Where would that be?'

Edward paused. Would it be too much of a risk? 'Tianlipin,' he said finally.

Sally stared at him. 'Surely not?'

'The foreign media can't easily access my country.'

'But wouldn't we face a new set of dangers there? Your family, I mean. Surely the last place you'd want to be seen with me would be your home country?'

'Correct. You would have to be incognito. Hide in plain sight.'

'So where could you take me?'

'Not to the capital. Not anywhere near the palace. But to my private retreat near the summer palace.'

'You have a summer palace?'

'But of course.' He sometimes forgot how others might react to the vast wealth of his kingdom.

'I still have to run my business. Does your retreat have Wi-Fi and internet?'

'Good access, high speed. I'll have to work too.'

'As long as I have that I'm okay. People are used to me being out of the country working with clients. As far as my brothers will know, I'll have extended my time in Singapore. That's what I'll tell my staff too.'

'Good,' he said.

'That still doesn't solve the problem of getting me out of here.'

'We might need help.'

Her brow furrowed. 'Who could we trust?'

'My sister.' He and Jennifer had always shared each other's secrets and had each other's backs.

'She lives downstairs, doesn't she?'

'She's on her way here now from the airport. If needs be, she would be a valid cover story for you.'

'Your sister and I are both hoteliers.' Sally narrowed her eyes as her thoughts ticked over. 'At the gala you rather cleverly established a professional connection between us.'

'Unintentionally, yes. However, now it could work to our advantage.'

'As far as the media is concerned, I could be her friend, not yours.'

'Although we don't want your identity getting out at any time if we can avoid it.'

'We most certainly don't,' she said.

He hated having to keep her a secret. He had to find a way he could acknowledge her.

'Agreed,' he said.

'How do we do this?' she said. 'I'm on a two o'clock flight to London from Changi.'

'Cancel it.'

'My stuff at the hotel?'

'Give your key card to my sister and she can organise someone to clear your room and pack for you.'

'I should do that straight away,' Sally said. 'But first, I need my handbag. I have dry crackers to nibble on. Helps with the nausea. And if I could beg a cold mineral water, please.'

'You don't want anything else to eat?'

'Not if we're travelling.' She paused. 'How are we getting to Tianlipin, by the way?'

'Our private jet,' he said.

'Of course we are,' she said drily.

'We'll take off from Seletar Airport. It's not far from the city and more private.'

'Right,' she said. 'If you can point me towards the living room, I'll retrieve my handbag.'

He put a hand on her arm to stay her. 'It might be an idea to dress in something more than the towel.'

She blushed, warm colour flooding her cheeks. 'Oh,' she said.

'Not that I don't think you look enchanting in just the towel. Or that, given other circumstances, I wouldn't be pleased to strip you of the towel and—'

To his surprise she laughed, wound her arms around his neck and kissed him firmly on the mouth. 'There's nothing I'd like better,' she said.

The towel fell off her and for a delightful few seconds he had sexy, naked Sally pressed against him. He groaned as his body responded.

'I know,' she said. 'I feel like groaning too. But we really don't want your sister to find us like this.'

'No, we don't,' he said.

Sally stepped back and immediately he felt bereft.

'How about you help me retrieve my clothes?' she said. 'After all, if you remember, you were the one who tossed them every which way.'

He remembered all right. And, despite the nerve-racking circumstances of the trip to Tianlipin, he was very glad he wouldn't be saying goodbye to Sally today.

CHAPTER EIGHT

SALLY PEERED THROUGH the window of the royal family's private jet as it prepared for landing.

Tianlipin.

Edward's country was spread below in a prosperous patchwork of green cultivated fields, rivers and lakes, natural forests, modern cityscapes, and everywhere the curved roofs of ancient temples and monuments.

'Why had I never heard of your country before?' she asked Edward's sister Jennifer, who sat opposite her on the luxurious sofa-like seating. Edward was in the cockpit in discussion with the pilot. Even their trusted staff had to believe she was Jennifer's friend and had no connection to Edward.

'It's a low-key destination,' Jennifer said. 'Mass tourism has never been encouraged. It's really only the intrepid traveller who finds us. Many want to keep it that way.' She paused. 'To be honest, I love my country but it can be a little dull for young people, which is why my brother and I both spend so much time in Singapore.'

'Won't that have to change one day?'

'You mean when Edward ascends the throne? My father is fit and healthy so we're hoping that won't be for a long time.' Sally thought she detected a note of reprimand in Jennifer's voice. There could be no doubt there was something different about those born to rule.

'Of course.'

'In the meantime, Edward's brilliant at heading the telco business and I've grown the hotel portfolio faster than anyone could have imagined.'

'Did Edward tell you I'm—?'

'A Harrington from the Harrington Park family? And sister of Hugo Harrington, boutique hotel chain owner and a competitor of mine. Not that I've ever met your brother. He's an elusive kind of guy. Clever and canny with it.'

'Yes, Hugo is all that,' Sally said with a surge of pride in Hugo that surprised her.

'I was considering a bid for the Harrington Park, but your brother beat me to it.'

Like he'd beaten her and Jay, Sally thought. Not that she'd share that kind of information outside the family. *Family.* Jennifer would be her baby's aunt. She might have to rethink her idea of family.

Sally had liked Princess Jennifer straight away. As she'd liked her brother straight away. Edward's sister—younger than him by a year—was whip-smart, forthright and incredibly efficient. She was also stunningly attractive, perfectly groomed and stylishly dressed in designer clothes from top to toe. Her black hair was pulled back from her face in an elegant high ponytail and she was perfectly made-up. That she bore a strong resemblance to her brother automatically endeared her to Sally.

Thanks to Jennifer, the escape from Edward's house had gone without a hitch. She had dressed Sally in one of her own long-sleeved, high-neck dresses, tucked her hair right up under a wide brimmed hat, applied heavy make-up and painted Sally's mouth with a shade of strong red lipstick she would never normally wear. 'I look so different,' Sally had exclaimed at her reflection in the mirror, fighting an urge to wipe off the dark lipstick.

'That's the idea,' Jennifer had said. 'If you shrink right down in the car seat as we leave, no one should see you. If anyone does catch a glimpse, they might think you're one of my friends. But they'll be watching for Edward and his mystery woman, not for me.'

The car had driven her and Jennifer to the jet waiting for them at the airport. The women had waited nearly an hour for Edward while he made sure he wasn't followed. When he'd finally arrived the three of them had been exhilarated by their success, with much relieved laughter and high-fiving.

But that exhilaration had worn off for Sally, to be replaced by trepidation. Her life had changed so dramatically in the space of twenty-four hours and she was pedalling frantically to keep up.

'You okay?' Jennifer asked.

'A little nervous.'

'Don't be. We'll work it the same way. You and I get off the plane together and head for the bachelor house.'

'The *what*?'

'It used to be called that years and years ago by my decadent twin uncles. Heaven knows what went on there then. I dread to think.' She shuddered. 'Anyway, Edward appropriated it for himself when he was at uni as a quiet place away from everyone else for him to study. I'll stay with you there until he arrives.'

And then Sally would be alone with Edward for who knew how long. The more she was with him, the more she would want him, the more painful the inevitable parting would be.

'Thank you for your help,' she said.

'Scandal averted and that's a good result. You have brothers. I'm sure you would do all you could to help them too.'

'Yes,' Sally said.

Would she? For Jay, it went without saying. But Hugo? Her cooperation with his plans for the hotel had been grudging at best. The problem was she didn't know her older brother any more. And what if she made the effort to get to know him again, got to love him again, and he left her again?

There'd been too much loss in her life. Not just the people—her parents, Hugo—but her life at the Harrington Park and her childhood home in the grounds of the hotel. She'd known it only as a happy place—pre Nick Wolfe, that was. Everything had changed when he'd moved in. More so when she'd got booted out to boarding school.

Love led to loss. It was another reason she had to guard her heart against Edward. One part of her was singing with joy at the thought of being alone with him. The other was warning her not to let herself fall for a man who would ultimately leave her.

'Be kind to Edward,' Jennifer said, her voice lowered.

'Kind?'

'You're in a difficult situation and he's doing his best.'

'I… I didn't plan this.' She and Edward had straight away told Jennifer about her pregnancy. There had been no point in trying to hide it. Back at the house, Jennifer had brewed her fresh ginger tea, which had helped with the nausea.

'I know.' Jennifer's expression softened. 'My brother is an honourable man.'

'Yes. Yes, he is.'

'If circumstances were different, I think you'd be right for him. He looks at you in a way I've never seen him do with another woman.'

'Th…thank you,' Sally stuttered, not sure what else to say. She couldn't let herself fantasise about an ongoing relationship with Edward or she'd go bonkers.

'I've said enough,' Jennifer said briskly. 'It's up to you and Edward how you sort things out. Come on, get that lovely hair of yours back up under the hat. We're about to land at our private airstrip. There will be a driver waiting for us. Edward has one of his own cars parked there. He'll follow us in that.'

The subterfuge would continue even in his own territory. No one could be trusted with a secret of this gravity—her scandalous pregnancy.

An hour later, Sally stood facing Edward in the living room of his retreat. Princess Jennifer had left—with a warm hug and instructions on how to make ginger tea—and it was just the two of them.

'What next?' Sally asked.

Edward had his hands clasped behind his back. He was wearing a cream linen suit, much the same as he'd worn the day he'd rescued her from the pool, and a white linen shirt. He looked around him. 'Being here feels anti-climactic after the drama of our exit from Singapore.'

'How did you know I was thinking just that?'

'Because of the connection I've felt with you from the get-go?'

'Possibly,' she said.

She didn't want to go there. That kind of discussion could only lead down pathways she wasn't sure she wanted to follow.

He was to be engaged to a princess.

Instead, she looked around her. 'This is a fabulous place to hide out.'

His retreat was set on the shores of a large bay. The view was mesmerising. Limestone islands covered in tropical vegetation loomed out of a glistening emerald sea, tiny white-capped waves lapped up onto a perfectly curved white sand beach. The sky was blue with a scattering of white cloud. There wasn't another dwelling in sight.

'It's one of my favourite places to be in the world,' he said, looking out to sea through a wall of glass doors. 'I can never get enough of that view.'

He went over and opened a set of doors that opened onto a wide covered veranda. It wasn't as hot and humid as Singapore, rather a warm sea breeze drifted through the doors, bringing with it the scent of salt and sweet tropical flowers. The breeze set off a series of musical chimes hanging from the railings of the veranda.

'Your house is none too shabby either,' she said.

His retreat—the so-called bachelor house—was no humble beach shack, but nor was it a mansion. She thought it might date from about the nineteen-fifties. The architect had given a nod to tradition in the shape of the roof and the awnings but otherwise it was a spacious two-storey house beautifully designed and recently decorated in a very contemporary style of white with highlights of blue—and no expense spared. Glass doors and walls of windows made sure the view was the focal point wherever you looked.

'As a professional, do you approve?' he asked.

'Absolutely. It's beautiful. Although there are always a few tweaks I'd like to make to any interior. You must have a good designer.'

'I leave that to Jennifer. She has a team she uses for her hotels.'

'I like your sister a lot,' she said.

'She likes you too,' he said.

'I'm glad.' For the first time, Sally felt awkward with him. As if she were scrabbling for conversation.

'I hope she might get back to see us in the next few days.'

'That would be nice.' She meant it. 'How long do you expect we'll be here?'

He shrugged. 'Time enough to let the heat die down.'

'Can you quantify that?'

'No more than a week, I should imagine.'

'A *week*!'

She began to pace the room. 'I don't know that I can be here with you for that long.'

He frowned. 'Why not?'

She turned to face him. 'I… I don't want to get too attached.'

'To the house?'

'To *you*.'

Edward saw the pain and conflict etched on her face and felt an answering ache deep in his heart. He was already too attached to *her*—that horse had bolted.

'I get that,' he said.

He could make no promises. And, even if he could, Sally had clearly stated she did not want marriage. Did not need him. But he wanted the chance to convince her otherwise. And he would have to fight for it.

Now was not the time to tell Sally he intended to petition his parents to release him from the deal with Princess Mai. Because a deal was what it was—a cold-hearted business arrangement between two rulers, with their adult offspring like pieces on a chessboard. It had nothing to do with his welfare or happiness. Or indeed the Princess's. The more he thought about it, the more he fumed it was unjust. As yet, no official documents had been signed. It might not be too late if he could win his father over.

'We could try to stay away from each other,' he suggested. 'The house is big enough to do so.'

'No,' she said immediately. 'That would be even worse.' Her shoulders slumped and she seemed very alone in the large, high-ceilinged room.

'Come here,' he said, opening his arms. After a moment's hesitation she came to him. He drew her close and she snuggled in tight. She gave a huge sigh and relaxed against him. He tightened his arms around her, dropped a kiss on the top of her head. She was just where he wanted her to be. For a moment he allowed himself the fantasy that this was how it could be for them. 'I know nothing about pregnant women. But you must be tired and hungry. You didn't eat lunch on our jet.'

'I don't think I'll ever feel hungry again,' she said. 'Although the ginger tea your sister made me definitely helped. She said she left fresh ginger and lemons in the kitchen so I could make some more.'

'You can leave that to me,' he said.

'You can make ginger tea? Is there no end to your domesticity?'

He grinned and dropped another kiss on her head. 'Ginger tea is an excellent cure for a hangover.'

'So that's how a prince learned to make it.'

'Back in my student days,' he said. 'But some skills you never forget.'

She laughed and the sound warmed his heart. She pulled back from his hug but remained in the circle of his arms, looking up at him.

'Sounds like a useful skill to me when you're sharing a house with a pregnant woman.'

'I'll make ginger tea when you need it, but it's powerful stuff so only in moderation,' he said.

'You have to be careful of everything you eat or drink when you're pregnant.'

'Did you study that in Prince School too?'

'No. I did online research while I was waiting to join you and Jennifer. On the basis of my research, plain boiled white rice is good for you when you're nauseous. Coincidentally, that's what my mother and my *amah* fed me, with sugar sprinkled on top, when I was ill as a child.'

For a long moment Sally didn't say anything. 'That's very kind of you, thank you,' she said with a hitch in her voice. 'I… I didn't expect that.'

'I'm being practical. You need to eat,' he said.

She blanched. 'Not right now, thank you. I think I'd like to just sit down and take in that glorious view while you tell me the history of the "bachelor house". I'm more than a touch intrigued.'

He rolled his eyes. 'Trust Jen to have informed you about it.'

'Would you have told me?'

'I wouldn't want you to get the wrong idea about my retreat.'

'Now I'm even more intrigued.'

'Come out on the veranda; it's a wonderful place to look at the sea and think.'

He led her over to one of two white rattan sofas piled with blue and white cushions and placed to take full advantage of the outlook to the ocean. He settled her in the seat with the best view and sat down beside her. He thought again, as he had thought when he met her in the airport, how disconcerting it was to see her looking so different in his sister's floral dress and with so much heavy make-up.

He began. 'There was a time in the family when the heir to the throne—'

'The Crown Prince, like you?'

He nodded. 'He was given freedom to—well, basically to "sow his wild oats" as you English might say.'

'It's an old-fashioned term and not exactly in favour these days. But I get what you mean.'

'Things were very different then.'

'And the Princesses?'

'A very different story for them, believe me. They were kept closely under the eye of their mothers and grandmothers.'

'Why does that not surprise me?' she said wryly. 'So this was the Crown Prince's party house?'

'This part of the coast is where the elite of our country spend their summer vacations. Our summer palace was built here one hundred years ago as a vacation residence for the entire extended family. It's a private gated estate with our own beach. The palace is built in traditional style and is very beautiful.'

'Those were the elaborate gates we came through when I got here with Jennifer?'

'That's right. The bachelor house was built in the nineteen-fifties. The heir, and maybe his brothers or cousins, stayed here—a twenty-minute walk from the main house. Everyone turned a purposely blind eye to what they got up to.'

'Seducing women?'

'I'm sure the twin uncles took to the idea with gusto. The parties were reportedly wild. They had a habit of swapping identities to trick people.'

She wrinkled her nose. 'They must have been awful,' she said. 'The twins, I mean.'

'Never to me. They were the fun uncles who bought me and my sister outrageously expensive gifts that we loved and made a huge fuss of us when we were little. The King, in particular, must have had a good deal of personal charm to have got away with all his excesses. I could never tell my father, but I cried my ten-year-old heart out when my favourite uncle died.'

Edward had had consequent cause to loathe his uncles when he discovered the depths of the damage they had done to the country. And his arranged marriage was a direct result of their behaviour. But he couldn't forget how he'd loved them as a child.

'I guess no one's one hundred per cent bad or good. Except my stepfather, who was one hundred per cent bad.' Sally slapped her hand over her mouth. 'Sorry. Forget I said that.'

'Please tell me more. You've heard about my complicated family, but I know nothing about yours beyond what I saw on the internet.'

'I thought my family was complicated until I heard about yours. I might have to downgrade mine to a level below *complicated*.'

'I won't know how to grade them until I hear the story.'

'It isn't nearly as interesting as yours, I assure you. Seriously, how could I possibly top the drama of your uncles?'

However, her story might help him to understand her better—and the family his child would be born into. 'I doubt anyone could. But you might surprise me.'

'First, I want to ask you something more

about the bachelor house.' She bit her bottom lip, couldn't meet his eye. 'Have you…have you brought a lot of women here?'

He stared at her, uncomprehending for a moment. 'You're the only woman I have ever brought here. Apart from my sister, of course.'

'Seriously?' She looked surprised but pleased in a relieved kind of way.

'My father's reign is a very different one to the monarch who preceded him. He let it be known he did not approve of their immoral ways. No bachelor houses under my father's rule.'

'So how did this one become yours?'

'When I was growing up, there was a lot of pressure on me to excel academically. Study didn't come as easily to me as sport. The sports I was permitted to play, that is.'

'There were restrictions?'

'For security and safety reasons,' he said. 'No team contact sports, for example, or dangerous pastimes like skydiving. Not for the heir to the throne of Tianlipin.'

'Sounds reasonable enough,' she said. She clenched her fists at the horrific thought of him crashing to earth in a skydive that went wrong.

'But I needed somewhere private to study,

without distractions. Sometimes the timetables and rituals of the palace became too much. When I was at university I asked my father if I could use the house when I wanted to barricade myself away from everyone and hit the books. An advantage was I could swim and sail here too.'

'So it went back to being the Crown Prince's retreat?'

'But a very different kind of retreat, I assure you,' he said.

'I'm glad I'm the only woman you've brought here. It…it makes it easier.'

He kissed her on the mouth, swiftly and gently. She kissed him back, with an air of quiet desperation.

Their kisses were running out.

'There's nothing easy for us about being here,' he said. 'But I like having you to myself even… even if it's only for a limited time.'

Sally sat back against the back of the sofa. 'You did have girlfriends, right? You just didn't bring them here?'

'No one serious until the second year of my undergraduate degree at university in Singapore. It wasn't easy for me to date. There was no hiding who I was, what my destiny was. Women were either too nervous to talk to me or had expectations I wasn't able to fulfil. It could be isolating.'

'Did your family vet who you were allowed to date?'

'Always,' he said shortly, unable to keep the bitterness from his voice. 'My university girlfriend was deemed unsuitable. Her parents were paid off, she was removed from university and I never saw her again. I took care about who I dated after that.'

There had been women who had been happy to accept a discreet no-strings relationship. But there was no need to go into the details of them for Sally. Like he didn't want to know about any boyfriends who had come before him.

'Did you often go incognito, like…like you did with me?' The break in her voice belied the coolness of her question. 'You know, pretending to be someone else?'

'Never,' he said vehemently. 'What happened with you was unexpected, spontaneous and totally without precedent. There was something so open and non-judgmental about you that my usual barriers fell away. With you I was myself. Just Edward. Not Crown Prince Edward. Not future King Edward. And you accepted me at face value for who I was. Not what I could do for you. Not for what you could get from me.'

She cleared her throat. 'You did give me a very nice dress. It fitted perfectly, by the way.' He was beginning to notice she had a habit of deflecting a conversation that got too close to any emotional truth.

'I wish I'd seen you in it.'

'After I got back to my hotel I contacted the boutique and tried to pay for it. But they refused to reverse the sale on your card.'

'Quite rightly. I wanted to help you. I told you at the time I didn't want you to pay for it.'

'I took the dress back to London. But I… I couldn't bear to wear it again. I was having so much trouble forgetting you and it brought back too many memories And yet I couldn't bring myself to throw out the dress. It's shoved to the back of my wardrobe.'

He hadn't just given her a dress that night. He'd given her a baby. And he needed to make very sure he kept both Sally and his child in his life.

In the meantime, he had to protect her—and himself—from a scandal that could be ruinous to them both if it erupted.

CHAPTER NINE

EDWARD GOT UP to get Sally a mineral water from the house and she settled back into the wonderfully comfortable rattan sofa. It was of an intricate weave pattern she hadn't seen before and she wondered if the furniture was made on the island. It would look fabulous in an English conservatory, perhaps even the conservatory that would follow in the winter wonderland space at the hotel. But she would not be doing business with furniture-makers in Tianlipin. She would want as little contact as possible with the reality of Edward married to another woman. Pain gripped her at the unbearable thought of him making love to anyone but her.

The ginger tea had settled her nausea, but she was still being cautious about what went into her mouth. She was running out of the dry crackers that had been sustaining her. Edward's plain rice might be a good place to start back onto regular food.

Who would have thought the Crown Prince would be so caring—and in such a practical way? But why should that be a surprise? She realised he had looked after her from the get-go—the *dim sum* in the hotel room, the dress, the comforting hugs. For all his powerful masculinity, his sometimes arrogant ways, there was something considerate about him, nurturing even. Perhaps that was the hallmark of a good ruler—one who looked after his people with a steady guiding hand. The people of Tianlipin were fortunate. He would be a good King.

He would be a good father.

She didn't want to entertain that thought and pushed it to the back of her mind to take up residence with all the other too-hard-to-face thoughts jostling for space. There was standing room only for recalcitrant thoughts since she'd discovered her pregnancy and Edward's true identity.

She suppressed a yawn. Not much sleep the night before and a rushed day was taking its toll. Being plucked out of Singapore just hours before she was due to fly home to London and then plonked down in this private paradise had been a shock, albeit with an element of excitement. To spend some time taking it easy might be a good thing as her body adjusted to the changes pregnancy brought with it. Next day she would get back to work. Brainstorming that elusive finishing touch to the winter garden was a priority. She also needed to fill Jay and Hugo in on her meeting with Oscar Yeo. She'd email them as she didn't want any awkward questions about why she hadn't flown home. There'd be enough awkward questions about her pregnancy to face later. She kicked off her shoes and leaned back to watch a brightly coloured traditional fishing boat tack its way across the horizon.

Edward returned with the mineral water, tall glasses filled with ice and slices of lime. 'Where does the mineral water come from?' she asked as he placed her glass on the table next to the sofa.

'The refrigerator. It's stacked with bottles.'

She laughed. 'It might have sounded like a silly question, but you tell me we're isolated here. How do we get food and supplies?'

He sat down next to her, stretching out his long legs, totally unselfconscious about his shoulders and thighs nudging hers. As if she belonged sitting next to him on his veranda. 'The summer palace is kept staffed all year around. I order what I want, and they deliver it here. Or a chef comes over and cooks for me. The housekeeping staff schedule visits to clean.'

'That's convenient,' she said. 'A different concept in take-away.'

How quickly she'd got used to the concept of him living not just in a palace but a summer palace too. And a bachelor house. Not to mention that elegant duplex in Singapore. Sally worked with some very wealthy clients, but she suspected they didn't come anywhere near the wealth of the Tianlipin royal family.

'But what happens when the staff see me here?' she said. 'How will you explain my presence?'

'They won't see you. You'll have to stay out of sight.' His tone was terser than she might have expected.

'You mean I literally have to hide myself? Like in a closet?' She couldn't keep the note of alarm from her voice. Was he serious? Her mouth went dry.

'I don't think you need to go that far. You can stay in one of the upstairs rooms behind locked doors.'

'If that's what it takes to keep the media off our backs, I guess I can find a crawl space somewhere to squeeze into.' She forced her voice to sound light-hearted, but she was appalled and more than a little angry at the idea of having to go to such lengths to conceal her presence in his home. As if she were someone to be ashamed of.

His scandalous secret.

She wanted to avoid the media discovering her identity as much as he did. But she knew it wasn't just because of the media interest she had to be hidden away while she was here. Jennifer had intimated that it would cause a royal uproar if her parents discovered he was keeping a woman in the bachelor house. Pregnant or otherwise—she would be seen as someone entirely unsuitable for their son. And risking his engagement. The thought that she might be considered inferior to him or anyone else made her feel a rising nausea of a different kind to morning sickness.

'Is it that you don't trust the summer palace staff?'

'I don't know them. The only staff I trust are mine, my security staff in particular. And the driver who picked you up from your hotel. They're my people, not my parents'—'

'Spies?'

'I wouldn't put it quite like that.' But the tone

of his voice told her that was exactly what he meant.

Her heart went out to him at having to live under such restrictions. Her heart also told her that she wanted a man who would stand up for her. Mr Edward Chen might be able to do so, Crown Prince Edward perhaps not.

He put a comforting hand on her arm. 'I'll make sure you don't have to hide for long. I'll keep staff visits to a minimum. They're forbidden to come here without my say-so.'

'Perhaps you could set off a warning when they approach to give me time to scuttle around and hide,' she said, hurt putting an edge of sarcasm to her voice. 'Like the air raid sirens in London during World War Two my grandmother used to tell me about. The Harrington Park stayed open right through the Blitz.'

'Fascinating to have that as part of your history,' he said, sounding genuinely interested and possibly relieved at a change of subject.

'My brothers and I recently discovered some marvellous photos in the archives of the entertainment they used to put on. It must have been terrifying to stay in London while the city was being bombed, but the hotel escaped damage.

My grandmother said they were doing their part for the war effort by keeping up morale, even though it was a financial strain.'

'Which grandmother was that?'

'My father's mother; she died when I was a teenager. The hotel has been going for more than a hundred years and was always until recently in the hands of our family.'

He frowned. 'Tell me what happened there, how you lost your hotel. It doesn't make sense.'

Sally paused, looked at him with her head tilted to the side assessingly. 'I'm not sure I should be talking about the hotel with you. After all, your sister is a competitor and by extension so are you. My brother Hugo would be furious with me if I spilled any beans I shouldn't. He owns it now, you see.'

'Now you've really got me interested. Not in the confidential business dealings of your hotel, but in what happened to you as a family that you lost something so important to you.'

He sounded genuinely interested, which was understandable. If he used terms like 'blood of my blood' he would want to know about the family that had donated the other half of his child's genes.

She looked down at her hands where they lay in her lap. Jennifer had painted her nails for her in a similar deep red to the lipstick. Sally was proud of how good they looked, although she would normally choose a paler colour polish. She'd started biting her nails after her mother died and she'd been sent to boarding school, away from the only home she'd known. It had taken her years to get out of the habit. But she'd never got over the sense of loss and isolation that had led to the nail-biting.

'You're right; the hotel was important to us,' she said. 'More important, perhaps, than we realised until we lost it.'

She took a sip from her water to avoid his too intent gaze. 'I don't like to talk about the past. It…it makes me uncomfortable.'

'Not as uncomfortable as it was for me telling you about my wicked uncles.' He paused. 'Sometimes the past is better confronted.'

'I'm not so sure about that,' she said, as always reluctant to talk about herself and certainly not the darker episodes of her life.

Edward swivelled to come closer. 'That grandmother you told me about?'

'Yes?'

'She was our baby's great-grandmother. I have a connection. I need to hear the story.'

She couldn't help but smile. 'And the twin uncles were the baby's great-uncles.'

'Let's hope he or she doesn't inherit their wild streak,' he said.

As if he would be around to see it.

'Perhaps a touch of feistiness if it's a girl. Girls need it in this world.'

'Did you need it? Was that because of what happened with the hotel?'

Sally swirled the ice cubes in her glass, conscious it was a delaying tactic. She sensed his need to know more about her. She had never talked about how she felt about her past life to anyone but Jay. But Edward was her baby's father; perhaps he had a right to know about the family she came from. She put down her glass.

'The Harrington Park Hotel wasn't just part of our lives for my brothers and me; it *was* our life. Our house was in the grounds of the hotel and Jay and I were in and out of the hotel from when we could toddle. We weren't allowed to get in the way, but the staff always welcomed us and gave us little jobs to do while keeping an eye on us. I remember when I must have been about five, being allowed to perch on the shiny wooden reception desk and hand the big old brass door keys on heavy embossed brass tags to the guests when they checked in.'

He smiled. 'They must have been enchanted by you.'

'I don't know about that, but I do remember feeling terribly important and pleased with myself. We each felt like we were contributing, although of course we didn't really understand what that meant. But we knew we belonged. We were Harringtons. Our hotel had the same name as we did and to be a Harrington was something to be proud of. Hugo was seven years older than us and he got to do real work, like deliver special requests to guests and help the porters. The hotel was very grand—'

'I remember. Very posh, very traditionally English.'

'But it was also warm and welcoming. My family's vision was to create a home away from home for our guests. They returned year after year, generation after generation, because of the sense of being part of the Harrington family experience, children included.'

'Nice,' he said.

'Don't steal our vision for your hotels,' she warned him, with a mock wagging of her finger.

'No need to worry,' he said very seriously. 'That kind of spirit is impossible to replicate. It has to come from the heart.'

'My father, Rupert Harrington, had a huge heart. He grew up in the same house we did and had the same connection to the hotel. My grandmother used to tell me he was born with hospitality flowing in his veins. My mother, Katherine, had stayed at the hotel as a child. When as an adult she met my father at a friend's party, she remembered him being kind to her when she got separated from her parents in that big hotel and he found her, lost and crying. The way she put it, she'd fallen a little in love with him back then, at eleven years old. The hotel was special to her too.'

'That's a very appealing story.'

'It is, isn't it? I used to ask Mummy to tell it to me again and again. How did your parents meet? I suppose they had an arranged marriage?'

'Actually, they didn't. They met as the children of family friends but never took any notice of each other. Years later, they encountered each other again at my father's graduation and fell in love.'

She looked down at her hands again. 'So they had a love-match, but you have to marry someone you don't even like. That doesn't seem quite right.'

'Yes, but my father was the third son and never expected to become King. I am the only son and Crown Prince. My marriage therefore assumes more strategic importance.'

And she wouldn't bring alliances or trade deals. Sally had to keep reminding herself of that every time she started to feel more for him than was wise.

'It's hard to imagine our parents as children, isn't it?' he said. 'It seems my father must have been born stern and strict. I think of him wearing his glasses even as a baby, but I know that wasn't so.'

'My father was jolly and generous, and I couldn't imagine him ever being any different. He particularly loved Christmas. Christmas at the Harrington Park was magical. His grandfather had started a custom of having a big Christmas tree in the lobby and inviting staff and guests to join the family in decorating the tree at a party on Christmas Eve. The way my mother put it, my father wanted to have the biggest and best Christmas tree of any hotel in London. His Christmas trees soared to the ceiling. We three children were allowed to buy a special ornament each year to hang on the tree.'

'You must have loved that. Christmas isn't a big celebration in my country, although it's getting more popular. But I'm sure you noticed it's a big deal in Singapore.'

'It was a big deal for us. My earliest memory is of my father lifting me up, safe in his arms, so I could hang my ornament high on the tree. Every year I can remember, I hung the first ornament.'

'He sounds like a generous, kind man.'

'Oh, he was. Every member of staff was given an ornament to hang. And each guest who stayed at the hotel on Christmas Eve found in their room a hand-decorated bauble with the hotel logo and their name on it. With it was an invitation to attend the party and either hang it on the tree or take it home with them. Many opted to join the party and hang their bauble on the tree, along with ours and the staff's.'

'That's a very clever marketing device,' Edward said. 'Those guests would have felt a real connection to the hotel.'

'He didn't do it with marketing in mind. According to my mother, it was instinctive and motivated purely by love and generosity.' She swallowed hard against the lump in her throat. 'I adored my father and wish I had more memories of him. But…but he died when I was six years old.'

'I'm so sorry, Sally,' Edward said, drawing her into a hug. She snuggled closer. Being close to him was like an addictive drug. Getting over the Edward habit would be way, way harder than conquering a nail-biting habit. Especially with his child in her heart as a constant reminder.

'It was a heart attack, sudden, unexpected. At six I barely understood what had happened. Just that he had left us. My mother went to pieces. And our lives changed irrevocably.'

For a long moment Edward held Sally close. She had become so important to him. He ached to comfort her. To assure her he would always be there for her. But that would be making promises he couldn't keep—*yet*.

No matter what happened with Sally, he knew

he would fight against a marriage to Princess Mai, indeed any arranged marriage. He wanted to be free to offer marriage to Sally. Not because of obligation because she was pregnant, but because he was already halfway to being in love with her. She gave no indication she might be feeling the same, but who knew what might develop as they spent more time together?

He sat back against the sofa. 'So where did the one hundred per cent bad stepfather come from?' he asked.

'Nick Wolfe. I shudder at the thought of his name,' she said with an exaggerated shuddering. 'He was an American businessman, a regular at the hotel.' She paused. 'Obviously I was only a young child when Nick made his move on my mother. My knowledge is based on not just my memories but stories from both my grandmothers—each who loathed him—and my older brother Hugo. He also, as it turns out, had real reason to loathe him. But that's another story. Hugo's story.'

'I want to hear your story.'

'I know. Forgive me if you have to drag it out of me.'

He got up from the sofa and reached out his

hands to her. 'We both need some fresh air. Come for a walk along the beach with me. I always think more clearly there. Something to do with the negative ions of moving water.'

She took his hands and let him help her up, not that she needed help; she just liked it. 'I'm not dressed for the beach. I'd like to change. I actually feel uncomfortable in this dress. It's because I'm a designer, I think—or maybe a control freak.' She gave a short nervous laugh. 'I can't bear to be wearing the wrong colour or shape; it makes me feel edgy. I'm so grateful to Jennifer for helping me with a disguise but I never wear florals or fussy necklines. And the dress is too short.' She put her hand to her cheek. 'Then there's this gunk on my face.'

From growing up with his sister, Edward knew he had to carefully consider his answer. It could go so very wrong. He decided to go full diplomacy. 'Whatever you think,' he said.

'What do you think?'

Was this some kind of test he couldn't study for? The truth could be his only answer.

'I like the shortness of the dress because it shows off your fabulous legs. But as for the rest of it… I agree. The dress doesn't suit you and you don't need that much make-up. That said, I think you look beautiful because you look beautiful in anything. And particularly beautiful in nothing at all.'

She laughed and gave him a swift hug. 'Thank you. So you don't mind if I pop upstairs and change? Jennifer put me in one of the guest bedrooms when we got here ahead of you.'

He wanted her sharing his bedroom.

He wanted her sharing his life.

But he wouldn't presume anything.

'Sure. Go ahead. I'm not going anywhere.' Not until he got her settled here and then made a visit to the city to present his case to his parents for release from any engagement plans to Princess Mai.

Edward barely had time to shrug off his jacket and check his phone for messages before Sally was back. She seemed to float towards him in a multicoloured silk kaftan that fell below her knees, teamed with simple strappy sandals. Her chestnut hair swung loose and the heavy make-up was gone. He caught his breath at how lovely she was. How much he wanted her.

'Now I'm ready for the beach,' she said.

It was only a few steps down from the veranda over the grass and onto the sand. Edward breathed in the salty air. Here he always felt a certain freedom, away from ever-present staff and scrutiny. The security people watching the bachelor house were hand-picked by him and trustworthy. Here he could be Edward Chen more than anywhere else. And this time here with Sally made it even better.

He walked along the edge of the sand with Sally as she also took deep breaths and exclaimed how wonderful it was. 'I love those traditional fishing boats traversing the bay,' she said. 'What are they fishing for?'

He laughed. 'I don't know what they're pretending to fish for but they're actually high-powered surveillance craft guarding the bay. There is also security posted at the top of the driveway to the house. They're my people so I don't have to hide you out of sight for fear of reports going back to the palace.'

Sally snatched her hand to her heart. 'You mean you're in danger? Are *we* in danger?'

'No immediate danger. Ongoing security is part of life for us.'

'Has anyone tried to…to assassinate anyone in your family?'

'Not in my lifetime. But there have been a few bungled break-in attempts that were diverted.'

'My heart is racing at the thought of it. Even more reason no one knows you're the father of my baby. The baby of single mum Sally Harrington is unlikely to be a target for kidnapping or…or worse.'

'Highly unlikely.'

He purposely downplayed her fears. Under the benevolent rule of his father, the elected people's advisory council, and with the high standard of living enjoyed by his subjects, there were few dissenters. But there was always the chance of some disgruntled rebel taking a stance. Sally and her baby needed to be under the official protection of the royal family, one way or the other.

'It's another thing for me to think about,' she said and went very quiet, her head down, as they walked side by side. Finally, she looked up at him. 'That really makes me all the more determined to raise my baby on my own in London with only minimal contact with you. I won't change my mind about that.'

'I won't argue with you,' he said, for the first time being less than honest with her. He couldn't tell her of his plans, not until he got the result he wanted. But he would never let her be in danger, no matter what he had to do to secure her safety.

Could she ever love him?

They walked until the end of the beach and then turned around. 'Do you swim here?' she said in an obvious effort to change the subject.

'Every day if I can,' he said. 'I learned to swim at our other beach in front of the summer palace.' He looked down at her. 'Why didn't you learn to swim?'

'I did learn. Well, I had lessons. Not very successfully as it turned out. Shivering in a cold-water pool with a bullying teacher striding up and down the edge yelling at us didn't exactly enthuse me. Swimming was not a favoured extracurricular activity—I'd far rather have gone to an art or craft class. Then when I became a boarder at my school—' She stopped.

'You didn't enjoy boarding?' he prompted.

'That takes me back to the one hundred per cent hateful stepfather,' she said.

CHAPTER TEN

SALLY FOUND THAT once she'd started telling Edward the history of the hotel and how the Harringtons came to lose their heritage, she felt compelled to continue. She was surprised to realise this was not so much for his sake, but for her own. Talking about what had happened for the first time with anyone other than Jay was making her see things more clearly, as if a fog was lifting from the well-worn memories.

Her actor ex had accused her of 'lacking the interpersonal skills to make emotional connections and commitments'. It had sounded like so much actor talk to her at the time and she'd coldly shut him down. He'd changed the rules and started to press for love and commitment she didn't want, *couldn't give.* But she was going to become a mother and had to be able to open her heart to love. Sometimes, in those dark hours when she wrestled with insomnia, she doubted she was even capable of love.

She'd never been outgoing like her twin, but somewhere along the line that little girl, darling of the hotel staff, focus of the love of her family, had grown into someone who had put her feelings into lockdown. Deep down, she knew her Ice Queen name was deserved, but how had she got that way? It went beyond a naturally reserved nature. Spooling through the story of her childhood was making her wonder if she had let herself be defined by loss and events out of her control.

There had been so much loss: her father, her mother, who she had loved but who had forced her to live with an emotionally abusive stepfather, her grandmothers, her older brother, her schoolfriends at a formative time, her soul-deep identity as a Harrington. No wonder she protected herself from further hurt. Locking down her emotions was something she could control.

Until now. Edward had been the first to breach her hard-set barriers. Edward, the only man to thaw the Ice Queen on that one glorious night, to get a glimpse of the real Sally Harrington. Edward, the man she was teetering on the edge of falling in love with but had to keep pulling herself back from that edge because, in his own words, a relationship with him was *impossible.*

'So tell me about this wicked stepfather,' he said. They'd reached the other end of the beach now and turned back towards the house.

'Wicked? That's another good adjective for him.'

'So far we have bad, hateful and wicked.' Edward checked them off on his fingers. 'I'm guessing there might be even more labels we can attach to him.'

'We could add greedy,' she said. 'Oh, and opportunistic.'

'Two more to add,' he said. 'I imagine the words carved onto labels like the brass key tags from your hotel you described, hanging from his neck on a chain like prisoners wear and weighing him down.'

'Great image,' she said with a grin. 'I'll only think of them like that now too.'

'I give you permission to use it,' he said.

Sally liked his unexpected whimsy. She made a mock curtsy. 'Why, thank you, Your Highness, I will.'

He caught her hand, suddenly very serious. 'Please don't call me "Your Highness". I only want to be Edward to you. Here, together, secluded, I don't want that other world to intrude on my time with you.'

She looked up into his handsome face, already so familiar. Again there was that feeling of unspoken words exchanged and acknowledged. 'Edward it is.' She reached up and kissed him on the cheek, rejoicing in her right to do so here, hidden away with him in his private retreat.

'Remember, just Edward.' He made a sweep of his hand as if he were indeed a king giving his subject permission to speak, but it was a gesture made in jest and with a smile. 'Please resume your story.'

'After my father died, my mother couldn't deal with running the hotel on her own, as well as caring for three distraught children.'

'It must have been difficult for her. The bigger the personality of a man, the bigger the gap they leave behind.'

She nodded. 'I'd never thought of it like that but you're right. There could only be one Rupert Harrington; he was larger than life. But Hugo Harrington had shadowed our father, as his natural successor. Another Harrington born with hospitality flowing in his veins. As he has since proved.'

Sally didn't want to reveal the cracks that had splintered their family, how their mother had so carelessly and inexplicably thrown away the legacy that was Hugo's birthright, how Hugo's resentment of their mother had smouldered over the years he had spent away from them. Not to a man whose sister was Hugo's competitor. But she could safely tell the surface story of the family his child would be born into.

'Surely Hugo would have been too young when your father died to play any significant role in the management of the hotel,' Edward said.

'Knowing what I know now, I reckon even at the age of thirteen he could have done a better job than my mother did, and certainly improve on Nick Wolfe's efforts. From the day that man took over, the hotel started its downward slide.'

'And you?'

'Me? Run the hotel? I never felt the calling. I loved it but I never wanted to make it my life. It was to be Hugo's.' When Nick had been declared bankrupt she had agreed with Jay they should try to buy it, but she had never seen herself as a manager.

'So when did the stepfather make his appearance?'

'Within months of my father's death he started insinuating himself into my mother's life. He appeared to be successful, charming. Maybe she thought he was someone she could lean on. But children are good at seeing people for what they are. Nick didn't fool Jay and me for long. He was attentive to us in front of our mother, but utterly indifferent when her back was turned. Hugo, being older, knew exactly what was going on. He wasn't afraid to voice it either, much to his detriment.'

In spite of the balmy air, Sally shivered. 'Nick Wolfe is not a man who should have been allowed close to children; he has a cruel streak. But just a year after our father died my mother married him.'

'Only a year? That was hasty.'

Of course Edward was shocked, as most people had been. She and her brothers had been horrified.

'I loved my mother, but I realised when I was older she was the kind of woman who couldn't exist without a man. She needed a man to lean on like a climbing plant needs a stake to cling to, losing her strength and ability to stand on her own in the process. After the wedding she wanted us to play happy families. She told us to call him Daddy. I refused. He was not my daddy and never would be. He said it was insubordinate of me to call him Nick. So I called him Mr Wolfe.'

'I imagine he wouldn't have liked that.'

'Especially when I continued to call him that for years after they were married. He saw it as a taunt, and maybe it was. I suppose it showed him up as a failure of a stepfather. Not that he had any interest in being a father to us. He wanted the hotel and he wanted my mother's inheritance from our father. Even as young children we could see that, but our mother never seemed to. Heaven knows what hold he had over her. My grandmother told me he flew into a fit of rage when he discovered our inheritances were held in trust and he couldn't get his hands on our money.'

'I'm beginning to see why you call him the one hundred per cent bad stepfather. One hundred per cent his other labels too. He sounds a very unpleasant individual.'

Sally stopped, scuffed her sandal in the sand as she figured how she could put her thoughts into words. 'The sad thing, and I find it hard to admit even after all this time, is I wanted a daddy. I was only seven years old. At the beginning he pretended to want a daughter to impress my mother, which only confused me. I wanted him to love me and for me to love him back. I… I don't know what that says about me.'

'It doesn't say anything about you except you were a little girl in need of a parent, but an awful lot about him—none of it good,' said Edward, tight-lipped. 'How did he end up owning the hotel?'

She continued to walk beside him along the sand. Edward was right. There was something about the atmosphere that gave a new clarity to her thoughts about the past. Or maybe it was simply being with him.

'He manipulated my mother into letting him run the hotel on the pretext she could have more time with her children. He then proceeded to make drastic changes and dismantle one hundred years of Harrington legacy. Everything that was dear to my father he destroyed.'

'Why? What motivated him to destroy a successful business? Was there some kind of drive for revenge there?'

She shrugged. 'I have no idea. As far as we

knew, he had no connection to our family until he ferreted his way into our mother's affections.'

'Was he using the hotel as a front for something else? Or was it just sheer incompetence? If Jen buys a successful hotel, she's careful to implement change slowly and only where it's needed. Goodwill is such an intangible but vital part of a hotel's value.'

'I don't know the answers. I was just a kid. But even a kid could notice the changes. The guests did too and voted with their feet.'

'There are many excellent hotels in London for them to choose instead.'

'Including ones your family owns?'

'Yes,' he said simply.

The relaunched Harrington Park would be competition for his sister's hotels. Could she trust him? She had to be very careful not to reveal any competitive details. Certainly not her winter wonderland.

'Over the next few years, Jay and I gradually stopped visiting the hotel. Not just because of Nick himself but because all the long-time staff who had made such a fuss of us left. He either got rid of them or they resigned because they couldn't bear to see what he was doing to the

Harrington Park. One of the first things he did was cancel the traditional Christmas Eve party. That was seen as a tragedy, but he wouldn't listen to protests.'

Edward frowned. 'And your mother did nothing? Not even to protect her asset?'

'Worse than nothing. She didn't protect me; she didn't protect my brothers. The following Christmas she signed over ownership of the hotel to him. Actually gave him the deeds to the hotel that bore our name. The power balance shifted. We Harringtons became dependent on his so-called "generosity" to live in our own home. He doled out an allowance to my mother that was always laced with conditions. From her own money.'

'Not her own money if she had signed everything over to him,' Edward reminded her. 'Morally yes, legally no.'

'I think he convinced my mother he would handle the business and money side of things better than she did. She believed him; after all, my father had a brilliant business brain and she'd never had to worry. But even she must have realised it wasn't working out as she'd hoped. That's when my mother begged me to stop calling him Mr Wolfe and become more compliant, which I did very grudgingly indeed. He also managed to get rid of Hugo. We didn't see our older brother for seventeen years and our mother never told us why. She actually never saw him again—her firstborn son.'

'That really was a tragedy. I didn't know that.'

Nor should he. It was private family business. Sally cursed under her breath. 'I've said too much. After all, you're our competitor.'

Edward stopped her with a hand on her arm and turned her to face him. He cupped her chin in his hand, so she had to look up to him. 'I would never use what you're telling me for competitive advantage. You have to trust me on that.'

'Can I really trust you?' she said.

'My whole existence is based on honour. You are special to me. And you're the mother of my unborn baby. I would do nothing to harm you.'

Except break my heart.

The thought came from nowhere. Sally wouldn't admit to any truth in it. She'd known the score from the get-go. She couldn't allow her heart to get involved. The Ice Queen needed to direct her freezing breath onto inconvenient emotions that could only lead to pain when they said farewell.

'I don't trust easily,' she said. 'Perhaps you can now see why.'

'I'm getting the picture,' he said. 'The word "dysfunctional" springs to mind.'

She gave a short humourless laugh. 'An apt description. My brothers must have suffered too but they keep it to themselves. With Hugo gone, my family shrunk to my mother, Jay and me. Neither grandmother would come to the house. Nick stopped any pretence of caring for us and spent less and less time at home. Christmases were dismal, to say the least. Then…then my mother died when I was thirteen. In a car crash. She was on the way to a school function. I… I was waiting for her. Waiting and waiting. Until I got a call to the principal's office.'

Edward put his arm around her. She melted into his comforting closeness. 'What a terrible loss for you, on top of everything else.' She stayed close, letting herself believe he cared for her. But there were too many 'if only's in the way.

'It was the worst thing that had ever happened to me. Despite her sometimes inexplicable actions when it came to Nick, I loved my mother and we were very close. Her funeral was unendurable. But it was scarcely over when Nick made his next move.

'With no warning, not giving us time to grieve, he made Jay and I full boarders at our school, effectively locking us away from everything we'd known. He didn't let me take anything of my mother's, even sentimental things of no value to anyone but me.'

'I'm sorry that happened to you. It seems like inexplicable cruelty.'

'It was unnecessarily cruel. I hated being a boarder at St Mary's; I was so homesick. If it hadn't been for Jay being there too, I would have run away.' Was that when her insomnia had started? The nail-biting certainly had.

'What was your contact with your stepfather then?'

'Minimal. As much as I hated boarding, I was relieved to get away from Nick. He…he'd become borderline abusive.'

'So we add *abusive* to his list of labels.' Edward's voice was cold with anger on her behalf.

But she didn't tell him everything. As her body had matured, she'd noticed her stepfather looking at her in a way she hadn't recognised or understood. It had made her uncomfortable and frightened. She'd begged her grandmother to let her live with her during the school holidays. When she'd had no choice but to see Nick, she'd made sure Jay was with her.

'Where is your despicable stepfather now?'

Despicable. Another label to add to the list. Edward's idea of the brass labels weighing her stepfather down was strangely cathartic.

'Thank heaven he slunk off back to America for good. I need never see him again. I don't care if he's dead or alive.'

'I understand why you feel that way. But have you and your brothers made absolutely certain he, as your stepfather, can't have any claim whatsoever on you in the future?'

Fear gripped her heart with icy claws. She couldn't bear it if Mr Wolfe came back into her life in any way. 'He didn't actually legally adopt us, I know that. But thank you, I'll check into it on behalf of my brothers too.'

They were back at the middle of the beach, in front of the house. By mutual decision she and Edward turned onto the grass and followed the short path back to the house. They sat down on the marble veranda steps, warm from the sun, and faced the sand. It was so tranquil and unspoiled here on a royal family's private beach in a country she had never known existed until a few days ago.

When she spoke, she looked out to sea rather than at Edward. 'What I learned from all that turmoil was that I would never let myself be dependent on a man. I would never be like my mother. I would make the decisions that affected my life, no one else. I wanted to be my own boss, to run my own company and I'm proud of what I've achieved. I won't ever have to ask a man for money or for help. Rest assured, I will always put our baby first. I don't intend to marry and risk a step-parent for the baby and I will never let him or her be ill-treated by any person they should be able to trust.'

Would he take her words as a challenge?

'You say you're a woman who doesn't need a man.'

'That's not to say I don't want one. But not to run my life.'

He took her hand. 'I know how important your independence is and I admire you for it,' he said.

She sat holding his hand and wondered why he hadn't seen anything to challenge in her statement.

* * *

The shadows got longer and still Edward sat with Sally, holding hands on the veranda steps. Who knew the history of a hotel could hold so much angst for the family who owned it? That in all the machinations after the death of the patriarch a family had been split and a little girl left lacking in protection. Reading between the lines, he thought if it hadn't been for the support of a twin brother and caring grandmothers, Sally might not have grown into the strong, independent woman she had become. It was a credit to her character.

Possibly too independent. Her statement of intent painted her life as a woman alone and unable to accept love. Her heart was in desperate need of healing. He saw her as warm and loving, if she let herself be that woman. He wanted to be the one to help her. For her sake, for the baby's sake and for his sake. But she would have to open her heart to him first. He didn't want an arranged marriage. He wanted to be in love with the woman who became his wife—but she had to be able to love him back.

He realised she had been silent for a long time

and when he turned to her he saw her cheeks were wet with silent tears as she looked ahead to the horizon.

'Sally! What's wrong? I shouldn't have made you trawl through your unhappy memories and—'

'It isn't that.' She turned to him. 'You helped me look at those memories through a different filter. To realise how I grew too fearful to choose love and commitment in case I got hurt. But there's nothing much I can do about that. Because the only person who has ever seen my real self is Crown Prince of a country on the other side of the world who is promised in marriage to a royal princess.'

He squeezed her hand harder at a rush of answering emotion from his own guarded heart. 'I wish things could be different between us,' he said. He was determined to make that possible, but he had to be sure he was free before he said anything—and that to be with him was what she wanted. She would have to give up a lot to become his Princess.

'I wish you were just Mr Edward Chen, free to make your own choices, and that your royal responsibilities weren't so onerous. I wish we'd had that night together, then met again and discovered that we actually liked each other quite a lot beyond our incredible chemistry. That we had time to get to know each other before decisions needed to be made. I wish—'

'Why couldn't I be Mr Edward Chen for the time we're here? And simply enjoy my time with you. I meant what I said. No one has ever made me feel the way you do.'

'You mean forget all about your responsibilities and obligations?'

'For a few days? Why not? Mr Edward Chen might have to do some telco work. But the rest of his time can be spent enjoying the company of Ms Sally Harrington before he has to go back to being that…that other person.'

He stumbled on the truth of the proposed fantasy. But he wanted her so badly he had to grab what time together he could. Time for them to get to know each other, to be sure the feelings he had for her were strong enough to carry them through a lifetime. And that she had real feelings for him.

'And Ms Sally Harrington has an interior design company to run remotely. But for the rest of the time perhaps she can suspend reality and… and enjoy the time she has with Mr Edward Chen without thinking of the *impossibility* of Crown Prince Edward.'

'Shall we do it?' She held her breath for his answer.

'I'm voting for a yes.'

'A yes from me too. Even though I fear it will make my goodbye to you when we go back to live our real lives so much more painful.'

'I'm speaking selfishly but I would rather take that pain and those memories of you into that real life than not have those memories.'

'I… I feel the same.'

'I'm a strong believer in fate,' he said. 'There is a reason we have been brought together. Some greater purpose that we've created a child.'

She frowned. 'I'm not sure I believe that. But I fell in that pool and you rescued me. Now here we are in a private paradise where we can indulge in a fantasy of togetherness. And perhaps, just perhaps, our child might be destined to do something significant for the world.'

'I like that idea,' he said.

She slid her arms around his neck. 'I'm tired of talking, Mr Chen.'

'I can think of other ways to occupy your time, Ms Harrington.'

He looked intently into her face. His breath hitched. How could it be possible that she looked lovelier every time he saw her? Sally was a beautiful woman. But now he was starting to unravel the layers of her complex personality to find the core of this wonderful woman who had fascinated him from the get-go.

He kissed her and even their kiss felt different. Less frantic. Less urgent. More a kiss without time restrictions, to be savoured, a slow fuse to a rising passion.

'Do you think your security people in that cute fishing boat that isn't exactly a fishing boat might have their sights trained on us right now?' she murmured against his mouth.

'I would hope not but I couldn't discount it.'

'We should probably—'

'Go inside so I can make you some boiled rice?'

'Ha! I have to be certain you're joking before I make a response to that.'

'I'm joking. However, if you would prefer rice to—'

'The rice can come later.' She laughed. 'But let's go inside. Should I wave goodbye to the security people?'

'Please don't,' he said as he kissed her again.

She got up from the steps, trying not to break the kiss. He got up with her, but they didn't quite succeed and stumbled. 'Call that a fail,' she said, laughing.

'No kiss with you is ever a fail,' he said.

'You do know how to say the right thing—must be that diplomacy you learned in Prince School.' She slapped her hand over her mouth. 'Oh. No. Sorry, Mr Chen, I don't know where that comment came from. I was referring to a different person altogether.'

He laughed. She tucked her hand into his arm. 'Shall we move sedately into the house, so your security people think I'm just a friend and—?'

'You could never be just a friend,' he said fiercely. 'I want you too much. I couldn't bear to have you around and not have you.'

They made it into the living room. 'Perhaps not here,' she said. 'While there is a choice of comfortable couches on this floor, there are also a lot of windows.'

'I shall have to carry you up the stairs then,' he said. 'My bedroom or yours?'

'Whichever we get to first, Mr Chen,' she murmured.

CHAPTER ELEVEN

SALLY KNEW SHE was existing in a bubble. But it was only too easy to put reality on hold and indulge in the fantasy that her lover Edward was just a regular businessman—albeit a very wealthy one to afford to live in this luxurious retreat.

But she was greedy, drunk on the joy of living day to day with him. She wouldn't let herself look past the next walk along the beach, the next kiss, the next joyous session of lovemaking that each time reached new planes of intimacy and mutual understanding of each other's needs.

She'd given up on holding herself back, of being cautious with her emotions, even though she knew the eventual pain of losing him would be horrendous. It was impossible not to fall a little more in love with him every day. Was he feeling the same? She knew he enjoyed her company, that he desired her was beyond doubt. But could it ever be anything more?

The morning, noon and night sickness wasn't easing; at times the nausea was debilitating. Edward constantly surprised her with his thoughtfulness and, yes, his boiled rice. She experimented to find other foods she could eat without adverse reactions and he ordered meals from the palace kitchens.

She and Edward fell into a routine of each doing essential work in the mornings, working around the time zone differences between Tianlipin and London, then spending the rest of the day together.

He insisted on teaching her to swim. The sea water was warm and buoyant, and Edward was a skilled teacher. Sally surprised herself by gaining more confidence in the water with every session.

'It's all thanks to my gorgeous teacher,' she said on the day she mastered the front crawl. 'I'm never going to love swimming though, you know.'

'Well done, Ms Mermaid,' he said. 'I won't always be there to rescue you if you get into trouble in the water.' The throwaway comment gutted her, but she refused to dwell on the truth of it—that she would be without him in her life.

She became fascinated by Tianlipin and begged Edward to show her some of his country. Twice Edward took her out in a car he borrowed from his security people, on the proviso she wore a scarf that completely covered her hair and obscured her face, as well as dark sunglasses. To go into the capital would have been courting disaster. But he showed her the elegant summer palace from a distance and drove through some of the nearby villages and small towns.

It was a beautiful country, blessed with an excellent climate, prosperous and orderly. She loved the tropical plants with their exuberant foliage and exotic flowers that grew only in greenhouses back home in London.

'I wish I could see more of your country,' she said, perhaps thoughtlessly, when they got home from the second trip.

'I'd like to show it to you,' he said. But she knew it wouldn't happen.

Not only was she interested in his country for her own sake, but Tianlipin would be her child's heritage as much as Britain would be. She decided to ask him a question that had been niggling at her. 'Why do you and Jennifer have such

English names? Surely you must have Tianlipinese names?'

'We have English names for the same reason my great-great-whatever grandparents changed to a Roman alphabet rather than Chinese-style characters. To be part of the greater world outside our island. It's also the reason English is taught in schools. Of course we go by our Tianlipinese names at home.'

'So tell me your real name,' she said.

'Edward is a real name, my Western name. My other name is Tian Zhi. In our language the family name comes first. So I am Chen Tian Zhi.'

She repeated it but stumbled over the pronunciation. He helped her until she got it right.

'Tianlipin means "gift from the sky"—my ancestors saw the island as a gift from the gods when they conquered it. My name means "son of the sky".'

'And Jennifer?'

'Her Tianlipinese name is Zhen Bao, which means "innocent jewel or treasure".'

'That's beautiful.'

When the time came, she would have to ask him for a Tianlipinese name for her baby.

* * *

The only blot on Sally's glorious existence was the need to lock herself in one of the unused bedrooms and keep quiet when the staff from the summer palace visited. She found it humiliating, as if she were a teenage girl caught out in her boyfriend's bedroom and forced to hide under the bed when his mother came in. Not that she'd ever been that teenage girl. She'd been a late starter in the dating stakes. And had never come anywhere near feeling for a man what she felt for Edward.

But she had a premonition that the outside world was about to intrude on their personal paradise. After a week of togetherness, Edward informed her he had to make a visit to his parents in the capital. She had a sudden irrational fear that he would never come back.

When Sally woke on the morning of his departure she found herself alone in his bed, the sheets still warm. She didn't panic; she knew he wanted to have an early swim before he left for the day.

She threw on her kaftan—so many times she'd been glad she'd packed it—and headed down to the beach. The sand felt warm under her bare feet and she revelled in the glorious view ahead of her. The early morning sunlight was dancing on the sapphire-blue water in sparkling starbursts, and she wondered how many places on earth could be this beautiful.

Edward swam back and forth along the length of the beach, his stroke graceful and powerful. He must have sensed she was there and broke his stroke to wave to her.

He swam towards shore then waded through the shallows to reach her where she stood on the sand. His black hair was sleek to his head, his body magnificent, the sunlight reflecting from the drops of water clinging to his powerful chest and shoulders. Sally caught her breath at a sudden rush of desire. She could never have enough of him.

'Is my mermaid joining me?' he called.

'Not this morning.'

As he left the water he shook himself and she was sprayed with drops of water. She jumped back and squealed. He laughed. 'You did that on purpose,' she accused.

'Of course I did,' he said. 'A mermaid shouldn't worry about a few drops of water.'

That led to Sally retaliating by running to the edge of the sand and scooping up seawater to splash him. The water fight was totally one-sided as he was already wet, and she ended up with her kaftan soaked. Laughing, she collapsed against his chest and conceded defeat.

He put his arm around her and led her back across the sand to the house. 'I need a shower, you need a shower. I suggest—'

'We shower together,' she said with a shiver of anticipation, knowing their shower would be an erotic as well as a cleansing experience.

After their shower, which was in every way as fun and satisfying as she could have imagined, Sally went with Edward down to the kitchen. With her kaftan hanging to dry, her sundress still in her suitcase as it was uncomfortably tight across her ever burgeoning bust, she wore one of Jennifer's sarongs, patterned in blue dragonflies, tied around her. Jennifer had told her she kept clothes here and to borrow whatever she wanted.

Edward was dressed in a perfectly tailored charcoal-grey business suit. He was heading off to a world in which she could never play a part. It made Sally, in her sarong, feel distanced from him. Edward Chen was slipping away from her.

No matter how much she grew to care for him—okay, to *love* him—she couldn't keep him with her.

'How are you feeling this morning?' he asked, considerate as always.

'I nibbled a few rice crackers before I got out of bed. It seemed to do the trick. I'm ready for a piece of toast with avocado now. And I'll brew some ginger tea.'

But, to tell the truth, she'd probably only take a few nibbles of the toast. The morning sickness wasn't easing. Despite the relaxed lifestyle, her fatigue wasn't getting better either. Edward teased her about how much time she spent napping. She was beginning to think she needed to see a doctor, but that wasn't an option for her here, where her existence had to be kept secret.

However, she didn't say anything to Edward. It wasn't that she wanted to play down her pregnancy. Rather she didn't want to bring up the contentious issue of the role Edward would play in the baby's life. He was destined to marry a princess. Sally was still determined to maintain her independence and bring the baby up by herself in London. If Edward was able to play some role in his or her life, that would be welcomed for the child's sake. For Sally's own sake, she would have to distance herself from him. It would be too heartbreaking otherwise.

Edward downed some coffee and glanced at his watch. While he was physically still present here with her, she could see his thoughts were racing ahead to the important meeting he had scheduled for later in the morning. He was flying rather than driving the four hours to the capital, he said, to minimise time away from her. Outside, a driver waited to take him to the airport.

'I'll be back as soon as I can,' Edward said. 'While I'm away keep the doors locked and don't let anyone in.'

'Are you expecting someone?' she asked, feeling nervous in spite of his reassurances she'd be fine there on her own.

'No, but we don't—'

'Want anyone to know I'm here. I know,' she said with a downward twist to her mouth.

'I'll miss you,' he said.

'Please don't talk like that,' she said. 'We can't be allowed to miss each other, not when soon—'

'You're right,' he said hoarsely. He dropped a lingering kiss on her mouth and then picked up his briefcase and headed towards the door.

Sally held up a hand in farewell. It was like a parody of a traditional domestic situation, the guy going off to work, the pregnant woman at home, she thought. That was the life her mother had wanted so desperately to maintain she'd married the wrong man and made life hell for her kids. Fun though it might be to play house-wife, it was not a real-life role to which Sally had ever aspired.

Then, with his hand on the door handle, Edward turned back. The look in his eyes echoed the feelings of despair and loss in her heart.

'Wait,' she said.

She rushed over to the door to kiss him, a brief, fierce kiss that she hoped conveyed to him how she felt. She hugged him close and he hugged her back, so tightly it almost hurt. 'Take care,' she said, her voice muffled against his shoulder. 'I'll miss you too. Terribly.'

She had a horrible fear she would end up missing him for the rest of her life.

CHAPTER TWELVE

WITHOUT EDWARD, THE bachelor house seemed very different. Sally wandered the empty rooms, admired the magazine-shoot-perfect décor, wondered what tales of decadent excess the white-painted walls could tell.

Even though she was a twin, she felt no affinity for the twin uncles and the way they had plundered the country they should have been honoured to rule. How different Edward's life could have been if his father hadn't had to step up, ill-prepared, to don a tarnished crown and restore its wealth and honour. As a result of the strict code of morality and honour the new King had imposed on the country, Edward was so duty-bound that his own needs and desires had been subsumed. But who was she to make that judgement? She'd never actually asked Edward how he felt about one day being King. The benefits of being a royal might far outweigh the strictures it brought with it. Only he knew that.

Mr Edward Chen was a fantasy and she knew she couldn't live in that bubble for much longer. Her staff were stepping up requests for a date when she'd be back. The client with the castle in Japan needed urgent advice on its restoration, and only Sally would do. Time was running out to complete the winter wonderland by Christmas Eve. But she thought she'd discovered the final elusive detail it needed—if her brothers agreed.

She settled herself on a white rattan easy chair on the veranda, in the shade of a palm tree beside a bank of potted orchids. Her conversation with Edward about her childhood at the Harrington Park had got her thinking about what she and her brothers really hoped to achieve from the relaunch. Not just in terms of furnishings and menus and the livery of the staff.

Her conversations with Edward had helped her to pinpoint it. What she believed they were seeking—consciously or not—was a spiritual healing by a return to the vision and values of the past. The hotel that bore their name and their father's name and their grandfather's name all the way back for more than a hundred years had been integral to their very being. Symbolic to that healing was the Christmas tree on which as children they'd hung their cherished ornaments in a ritual of celebration and continuity.

The focal point of her winter wonderland was a stand of fir trees, elegantly woven with fairy lights as a subtle nod to the festive season. But she realised now that it was too subtle and didn't invite any interaction with the guests. She'd let her own disdain for Christmas influence the design. Why not go all-out and put in an over-the-top tree like their father would have done? Then bring back the ornament-hanging ceremony. Include the staff. And restore the custom of the personalised baubles in the guests' rooms. Sally felt a rush of excitement. It could work. They still had time.

Hugo had employed his favourite event planner from New York, a woman named Erin, to work with him on the launch party. Perhaps Sally could liaise with Erin on the details when the planner arrived in London—if Hugo approved of the change.

Sally put together a detailed proposal for the change of emphasis and emailed it to Hugo and Jay. As she did so, she realised she hadn't actually spoken to either of her brothers since she'd left for Japan and then on to Singapore. She didn't want to give away anything of the truth of her situation with Edward. The relative anonymity of email worked fine. Jay was preoccupied with Chloe and she supposed Hugo was obsessed with the relaunch.

The morning flew as she caught up with her work. She realised she'd been neglecting her business and that the neglect had to stop. She had proudly boasted to Edward that she could support her baby by herself. But not without the very good income the business brought in. For all her ideals of independence, she had been only too happy to push everything else aside, save for the bare minimum of maintenance, just to be with him. Was that what falling in love was like? If so, she realised she had never before felt anything remotely like it. Until now.

As she made her way back to the kitchen, she heard a loud knock. Someone at the door. She froze. She couldn't be seen here. Where to hide? Dive under the kitchen table? Crawl to the broom closet? Barricade herself in the toilet? Her heart was pounding, and her mouth went dry. It sounded again. She looked around. It was just a small branch banging high on the kitchen window.

Sally slumped with the intensity of her relief. Of course no one would be knocking on the Crown Prince's door. That was what the security detail was there to stop. And yet her first reaction had been to hide in the most undignified manner. She hated the feeling it invoked in her. This went beyond avoiding media scrutiny. This was about her being subservient to the palace. She didn't like it at all.

She managed some poached chicken for lunch. It was delicious, sent over the previous evening by the summer palace staff. There again was subterfuge. Edward ordered food for one. One royal appetite requiring several courses. It was as if Sally had been blotted out of existence.

After lunch she went upstairs to 'her' room to lie down. Of course she slept in Edward's bed every night. Waking up spooned with him was one of the great joys of this interlude away from reality. But she felt the need for distance and chose the other room. She was so exhausted from the effort of doing not very much at all that she fell asleep immediately.

Sally awoke what must have been hours later to find Edward sitting on the side of the bed.

She started, then smiled drowsily at the sight of him. She stretched out her arms above her head as she struggled up through the layers of deep sleep. She was about to ask him how his meeting had gone when she noticed the glumness of his expression.

Immediately she sat up, the sarong barely covering her. 'What's wrong?' she asked. 'How did your meeting with your parents go?'

'My meeting with the King and Queen—remember they are my rulers as well as my parents—went dismally.'

'I'm so sorry to hear that,' she said, taking his hand and squeezing it in sympathy.

He sighed with a great heaving of broad masculine shoulders. 'I wasn't honest with you about the purpose of the meeting.'

She frowned. 'Not honest?'

'I let you think it was a business meeting. But it was nothing of the kind. Well, not in the straightforward business sense. I requested the meeting to lay down my case for not going forward with the engagement to Princess Mai.'

'Oh,' she said, her thoughts racing. 'Did you mention me?'

'No.'

Sally's heart plummeted. Again she had that feeling of being blotted out of his life. 'I see,' was all she could manage to get out from a constricted throat.

'I didn't want to complicate the issue by mentioning you. My argument was based on the unsuitability of Princess Mai, and that I shouldn't be forced into a marriage that might be good for the country but would not be good for me. That led to the argument that I am thirty-one years old and should be allowed to choose my own wife.'

'But…but you didn't talk about me, or tell them about the baby?'

'Would you have thanked me if I had without consulting you first?'

She shook her head. 'No. I… I would have been annoyed.'

'I've got to know you well enough by now to be aware of that.' He picked up her hand and dropped a kiss on it.

'It's actually two separate issues,' he said. 'My desire to refuse an arranged marriage to a particular princess and my desire to choose my own life partner. But the issue only came up because of you.'

'Because I'm pregnant?'

'Not because of that. Not solely. But because I've never felt about a woman the way I feel about you. How could I marry another woman? I'd rather not marry at all.' His dark eyes were warm with sincerity and conviction.

Sally felt as though all the breath had been punched out of her body. 'I... I didn't know.'

His mouth quirked. 'Don't worry. I'm not about to ask you to marry me. I know your thoughts on the subject.'

'I'm sorry. I couldn't—'

Panic seized her. To go from *impossible* to the possibility of *marriage* so quickly was too much to comprehend.

'No point anyway. They point-blank refused.'

'What? Did they hear you out?'

'They let me finish my petition—'

'You had to *petition* your parents?'

'I was asking for a change in a royal ruling. It had to be official. I'd thought it all out, written it down. Planned what I'd say while you were lying asleep on the sofa.'

'Here?'

'Yes.'

Who knew? Was this all about her being pregnant and him wanting to do the right thing by his future child? Would he have taken his petition to his parents the King and Queen if she hadn't been pregnant?

He got up from the bed and paced up and down the room as he spoke. His fists were clenched beside him and she had never seen his face set so grim. 'They didn't allow debate. The marriage is too important in terms of diplomatic and trading relations. If we renege, the loss of face to the Princess and her father would do irreparable damage to our country. The answer was *no*. No matter how I feel about it, they decreed I have to marry Princess Mai.'

'Did you point out that your father was allowed to choose his own wife?'

'Yes, but I was shut down immediately. He was not the Crown Prince at the time. That was reason enough that I do not have the same privilege.'

Mr Edward Chen had departed the room when he'd left this morning. Crown Prince Edward had returned. They were right back to *impossible*.

Edward had never felt more frustrated or angry as he railed against the absolute rule his parents had imposed on him. He had been the dutiful Crown Prince since he was ten years old.

But his desires meant nothing. He appreciated he lived a life of privilege. But how empty was the most extravagant palace without the right partner by his side? He'd accepted the need for an arranged marriage when it had been in the abstract. But that was before he had met Sally. He would not give up on this. There were further steps he could take. No matter the consequences.

Sally's face was pale with shock. Her hair was all mussed and her sarong had come loose, revealing rather more of her breasts than she might have been aware of. Not that he was complaining. She had never looked more beautiful. He had never wanted her more. But, before she opened her mouth, he knew what she was going to say.

'I have to go back home,' she said. 'It's time.'

She stood up from the bed to face him. He knew it was because she wanted to put them on a more even footing.

'I would rather keep you here with me,' he said.

'I know,' she said, her voice low and throaty with regret. 'I've loved my visit with Mr Edward Chen. But his other life is calling him, and I can't tag along.' Her voice broke. 'My life is calling me too.'

'I wish your life would be quiet,' he said in an

ill-judged attempt at levity. There could be nothing light-hearted about this conversation.

She listed her reasons for that insistent call to home. 'The media has moved onto the next big thing. My business needs my attention. My brother wants my help with the hotel.' Edward could barely comprehend her words he was so caught up in his own grief at the thought of losing her. 'And I need to see a doctor.' Those words came through loud and clear and he was instantly alert.

'A doctor? Why? What's wrong?'

'Nothing is wrong. At least I don't think it is. But I'd like to be reassured that this constant fatigue and nausea is normal. All the advice online says at this stage I should check in with a doctor anyway, who'll see me through the pregnancy and birth. I need to go home.'

'There are good doctors here.'

'I'm sure there are. But not for me. Because I'm not meant to be here. I'm not meant to be part of your life in any way. I… I don't like being your secret and having to hide my existence from your family. I can't live in someone's shadow, my every move judged as how it might affect you. I've hated having to hide when your staff is here. I've found it…demeaning.'

'I'm sorry,' he said. 'I didn't know you felt that strongly. I was trying to keep you safe.'

'I know your intentions towards me have always been in my best interest. Don't ever think otherwise.'

This time alone with her had meant more to him than he could possibly articulate. He'd wanted time to know for sure she was the woman for him—and he'd been given it. But to what purpose? 'There *must* be a way we can be together.'

Sally looked up at him, grey eyes shadowed. 'I wish there could be a way. But the gate has been slammed shut. Your meeting with your King and Queen made it—*us*—even more *impossible*. I suspect they won't let you delay your engagement to the Princess any longer. Even if the post of Official Mistress was open, I would never want to fill it.'

She turned and walked away from him, only to turn back on her heel to face him again. Her face was resolute and told him Sally was of the rip-the-plaster-off-quickly school. 'I have to leave here, Edward. Now. Or tomorrow. As soon as I can get on a flight from Singapore and you can get me there to board it. I have to go back to my independent life, for my own sake and that of my baby.'

Our baby, he thought, but didn't say. He wanted to take her in his arms and tell her that he was in love with her. But how empty were declarations of love from a man who could offer her nothing but words? Until he could behave towards her with honour and make the impossible possible, he had to let her go.

Did a heart shattering into little pieces make a noise? If so, Edward would be deafened by the sound, Sally thought. Telling him she had to leave hurt her more than she could ever have imagined. Thankfully, he didn't try to convince her to change her mind.

Over the years she'd become adept at keeping people at a distance, especially men. Even her friends were really no more than acquaintances. The only person who had any hold on her heart was Jay. They were twins, they'd been born having a hold on each other's hearts. But Edward was different. When she was in his arms he became her world.

She was in love with him.

She'd fought so hard to protect her heart but lost the battle. Although she could never tell him that. Because he, with all his talk of gaining his freedom to marry, had never said he was in love with her.

'Thank you for not making this any more difficult than it has to be,' she said. She steeled herself to sound practical because being organised, getting things done efficiently, was the only way she knew to get through this agonising wrenching away of her heart from where it ached to be.

'You book your plane home from Singapore,' he said. 'As soon as you tell me the flight details, I'll organise my jet to get you there from here.'

Their lives were spiralling apart already.

Sally had no more words. She lifted her face to kiss him. He kissed her back with a fierce desperation. She clung to him. Their time together was counting down, heartbeat by heartbeat. Soon kissing wasn't enough. Their lovemaking was thoughtful and considerate—they knew each other's needs well now. Yet the thought of separation made her reach for new heights of passion with a fierce desperation. She wanted to

tell him with her body what she could never say
with words.

Afterwards, as she lay in his arms, she determined that she would stay up all night. She
wanted to make the most of their last night together, even if that meant simply watching his
handsome, beloved face as he slept.

Of course she fell asleep, her head on his shoulder with his arms wrapped tightly around her as
if he could never let her go. When she woke
up, with a muffled cry of disappointment that
she had wasted those hours with him in sleep,
the sun was slanting bright through the shutters.
Time for her to leave the bachelor house. Time
for her to leave Edward.

He flew with her to Singapore on his private jet. She sat close to him, discreetly holding
hands. He was as quiet as she was. All that was
to be said about their impossible relationship had
been said. Still being careful to avoid gossip, he
stayed on his jet. She said goodbye to him with a
hug that could have been a hug between friends
if anyone were to witness it.

'Don't look back,' he said, his voice hoarse.

Sally was too choked to do anything but nod.

His Singapore driver was waiting to take

her to the passenger terminal at Changi. There she melded into the masses taking commercial flights from one of the busiest airports in the world.

Once through to her gate, she wandered around the shops to distract herself from her thoughts, barely taking in her surroundings. She was looking for something, but she wouldn't know what it was until she saw it.

The shops were decorated for Christmas. She stopped at a boutique, mesmerised by the Christmas tree covered in glittering ornaments that filled the window. Most of the ornaments were of the type she could easily buy in London: Santas, candy canes, bells and the like.

But then she spotted an elegant tree ornament in the shape of a Merlion, the mythical creature with the head of a lion and the body of a fish that was the symbol of Singapore. It was made from white porcelain strung through with a red silk cord and tassel. She had found the ornament she would place on the Christmas tree in her winter wonderland on Christmas Eve at the relaunched Harrington Park Hotel. She had to turn her thoughts homeward.

CHAPTER THIRTEEN

SALLY STAGGERED OFF the plane at Heathrow, London. The crowds of people waiting to greet loved ones from international flights had never bothered her before. Now she had to avert her eyes from the joyful reunions going on all around her—lovers kissing, families hugging. It was too painful to endure when she had been forced to say goodbye to Edward. She had never felt more alone. The only person she had waiting for her was a driver holding up a sign with her name on it.

Icy air hit her as she left the airport to follow the driver to the car, and she huddled into her coat. It was impossible to believe that just the day before she'd wandered around a beach house filled with sunlight in only a sarong and bare feet.

She didn't tell anyone she had returned to London. Exhausted, she stayed in her flat all day. Nothing could help her emotional exhaustion.

To finally find the man she knew she could love and then have to leave him through no fault of her own—or his—was an unendurable heartache. That she was pregnant with his child to love was a blessing.

But, despite her fierce protestations of independence, she knew it wouldn't be easy being a single parent. And that some kind of visitation rights would have to be negotiated if Edward wanted them. In reality, she expected instead that lawyer's letter from the Tianlipin palace asking her to sign away any claims on Edward and his family.

She did what she always did with such inconvenient thoughts—pushed them right to the back of her mind. But they wouldn't stay there; thoughts of Edward kept jostling themselves to the fore, insisting she acknowledge them and the impact he'd had on her life and on her heart.

Then he sent a text to say he hoped she had got home safely. Like a lovesick teenager, she hugged her phone to her heart, tears sliding down her cheeks. Already she missed him dreadfully. She had mourned her mother so deeply she had been ill with grief. But death was such a final farewell. This was a different kind of mourning. Edward was carrying on his life without her, about to become engaged to be married to another woman. But she knew he must be mourning her too. She had faith in what they'd had was real. Even if it couldn't last. Even if he had never actually told her he loved her.

Sally found it in her to feel a little sorry for Edward's future fiancée, especially if she became aware of how reluctant he was to go ahead with the deal. That was what he called it—a *deal*. There was nothing remotely romantic about his engagement. That wasn't to say she wasn't devastated at the thought of him with another woman.

She kept telling herself she'd get over him eventually, although the words didn't ring true even in her own mind. Life had to go on, as the tiny life inside her would grow. But, this soon in, the separation from Edward wasn't ever going to be easy.

She managed to get an appointment with her GP for two day's time. Next day, she headed into her office in South Kensington, a walk from her apartment. Her personal assistant expressed alarm at how unwell she appeared. Was it that obvious? Sally joked about food poisoning from her foreign travels and asked her to pop out to the shops and buy her dry crackers. It was disconcerting to note that no one even contemplated the thought that she might be pregnant. Not the Ice Queen who hadn't dated in forever.

Work that required her urgent attention had piled up. She should never have stayed away so long. Thankfully, her very able senior designer had stepped up to the plate, as had her business manager. As her pregnancy progressed, she would give them even more responsibility. In fact, she was considering making them partners in Sally Harrington Interiors.

Already, her idyllic time with Mr Edward Chen at the bachelor house on that glorious beach seemed a lifetime ago.

While she'd been away she'd been in constant touch with Oscar Yeo's London team about the progress of the winter wonderland. They'd sent photos daily. But she needed to eyeball the design for herself. She drove over to the hotel next morning. After all the time she had spent discussing the Harrington Park and its importance to her family with Edward, she wondered how she would feel seeing the building again—their hotel back in Harrington hands again.

Her heart lifted at the sight of the familiar façade, with its grand gates and portico. Having been away for nearly two weeks, she found the utter splendour of the building hitting her afresh. It was grandeur on an old-world scale—even with scaffolding still present on some of the external walls. The repairs and refurbishments were on a scale that she and Jay could never have afforded to do as well as Hugo with his vision and deep pockets. It was her older brother she had to thank for restoring the Harrington Park.

And yet she still felt distanced from him. Did Hugo care more about reclaiming the Harrington Park as some kind of revenge on their late mother and Nick Wolfe than he did about her and Jay? What would happen when the hotel was up and running again? Would he discard his siblings as readily as he'd done before?

Inside was a hive of industry, with tradesmen working around the clock on the renovations. The smell of fresh paint and sawn timber was familiar and exhilarating. The guest rooms were nearly complete. She inspected two and was very satisfied with the work the subcontractors had done. Seeing her design ideas come to fruition was a thrill that never got old. Hugo had set aside a makeshift office for her in an alcove in the ballroom amid the drop sheets and ladders and she placed her laptop down on the small table that acted as a desk.

Sally didn't know when she'd tell her brothers about her pregnancy, but it wasn't going to be now. She'd dressed carefully in an oversized cashmere knit top that fell to mid-thigh and stretched out leather trousers, to disguise her expanding waistline and bust. She'd breakfasted on dry crackers to fight the nausea and enable her to work. But nothing she did stopped a nagging headache she was finding hard to ignore.

Jay was in France, sorting things out with Chloe, Sally hoped. Her twin had called the heart-to-heart he'd had with her the last time she'd been in London a 'verbal slap around the head'. She was glad she'd spoken frankly with him, as she so wanted him to find the happiness that had eluded him with anyone else but his teenage love.

Jay was a one-woman man. Would Sally be doomed to be a one-man woman, forever comparing other men to Edward and finding them lacking? She honestly couldn't imagine dating another man—*ever*—after the joy she'd found with Edward.

Hugo greeted her coolly and a touch abruptly. She supposed he was annoyed she'd spent so long in Singapore. Little did he know the scandal she had averted, right at the time he wanted positive press for the relaunch of the hotel. She pasted a smile on her face. The last thing she wanted was confrontation. She didn't want to blurt out something she shouldn't have. Something that might betray Edward and the special, secret time they'd shared together.

Hugo had immediately approved her idea for the Christmas tree by return email back when she'd still been at the bachelor house. Jay had also been enthusiastic. Now, Sally found her way through the construction and down to what had been the courtyard off the foyer. And there it was—her winter wonderland, nearly complete, lake and all. She shivered, not just from the temperature-controlled chill and the snow spraying out from the artificial snow gun, but at how utterly perfect it looked.

Most importantly, the one huge fir tree—the Harrington Park Christmas tree—dominated the other fir trees. Like all the trees, it would be strung with fairy lights. But it would become the focal point of the garden when it would come to life with ornaments, tinsel and an abundance of seasonal goodwill. Somewhere there must be a store of ornaments from years gone by. She would make it her mission to find them.

The display was part of the hotel's relaunch, to what she and her brothers hoped would be a great commercial success. But the winter garden was also intensely personal to the Harrington family. Working with the contractors, she'd had the floor plan changed so there would be clear access for partygoers to hang their ornaments without slipping on the snow. She walked over, safe in her boots. The memorial plaque was in place.

In memory of the late
Rupert and Katherine Harrington
who loved Christmas.

A lump in her throat, Sally stood looking at it for a long time, remembering. The last time she'd hung an ornament on the hotel tree she had been six years old, held in her daddy's arms. Now, at twenty-seven years old, she could imagine herself on Christmas Day hanging her Singapore Merlion ornament on behalf of her unborn child. But she would be doing it alone, her baby's father far away in the country that demanded his unquestioning allegiance.

She headed back towards the upstairs ball-room, taking the grand marble staircase. The change from the freeze of the winter garden and the heating of the foyer made her feel giddy and she had to stop halfway and hold onto the handrail. Her head throbbed but she didn't want to take medication because of her pregnancy. She reached her little office and headed towards where she could see Hugo talking to a plasterer. But, as she approached him, she felt dizzy. It seemed as if the room was spinning around and around in a blur. As her knees started to collapse under her, she cried out to Hugo. She was aware of her brother catching her before she fell. And then nothing.

Sally awoke, heaven knew how many hours later, to find herself in a hospital bed in a private room. She was attached to both a drip and a monitor. Hugo sat in a chair by her bedside. 'Welcome back,' he said.

She tried to sit up, but the monitor buzzed and she lay back against the pillows. 'Wh-what happened? Why am I here?'

'You fainted. Gave me a terrible fright. I called an ambulance and they brought you here.'

'Oh. I don't remember.'

How like their mother Hugo was, she noticed, with the same chestnut hair and grey eyes. The same colouring as herself, in fact.

Then suddenly she did remember. Her hand without the monitor went straight to her tummy. 'The baby.'

'Perfectly fine. So are you. You were suffering severe dehydration and anaemia. You're on a drip. When were you going to tell us you're pregnant?'

'How…how do you know?'

'I came in the ambulance with you. I had to kick up quite a fuss to prove I was your next of kin and entitled to talk to the doctors about your condition.'

Hugo was her next of kin. It didn't matter how many years they'd been apart, he was her older brother. Nothing could change that. They were blood kin. Like her baby would be blood kin to Edward.

'Tell me about your pregnancy.'

Sally bristled. She would have told Jay straight away. He'd told her everything about Chloe and she would tell him all about Edward. But Hugo's request sounded more like a demand. 'That's actually my business,' she said.

'You made it my business when you fainted in my arms. Hell, Sally, your eyes rolled back in your head and I thought you'd died. Can you imagine how I felt?'

At the genuine distress in his voice, she softened towards him. 'Thank you for being there for me, Hugo. I'm sorry you had to go through that.'

'There's no need to apologise. I'm your brother. I'm glad I was there to catch you.' He swore. 'When are you going to forgive me for staying away?'

'Having you back takes some getting used to,' she said stubbornly. 'But I really appreciated you helping me today.'

'Did you *know* you were pregnant?'

'Yes, I did. It…it wasn't planned and came as quite a shock.'

'The father?'

'Someone I… I care for very much. But we can't be together.'

Hugo's face set grim. 'So he's walking away from his responsibilities?'

'It's not like that at all. I'm determined to be independent.'

'Is he—?'

She put her hand up in a halt sign. 'Please don't ask me any more about him,' she said. 'But thank you so much for helping me today. I… I'm very grateful.'

A nurse came in, wanting to take Sally away for further tests. 'Don't stay, Hugo,' she said. 'I'll be in good hands here. There's so much for you still to do at the hotel, with the relaunch only just over a week away. Please. You're needed there.' He went to protest but she spoke over him. 'I'll be worried if you're not there overseeing things. Please.'

He kissed her on the cheek, which surprised her. As she watched him leave she felt immeasurably sad. First because she had grown up without the brother she'd hero-worshipped and she was having so much trouble reconnecting with him. And second because in an ideal world it wouldn't be her brother accompanying her to hospital but the father of her baby.

After the blood tests and ultrasound were done, she was returned to her room. It all felt quite surreal that she had ended up in here. Like a dream, but not a particularly happy one.

The obstetric consultant was next to see her. The consultant's manner was brisk but kind. She explained to Sally that she was suffering from a condition known as *hyperemesis gravidarum*, an extreme form of morning sickness that caused excessive nausea, vomiting and fatigue during pregnancy. It was thought to be caused by excessive production of one of the hormones produced in early pregnancy, known as human chorionic gonadotropin.

Sally clutched a corner of the sheet so hard her knuckles showed. 'What causes that? Is…is something wrong with my baby?'

She smiled. 'Your babies appear perfectly normal.'

'Babies?' Sally stared at the doctor.

'You're pregnant with twins. And a multiple birth can be associated with that kind of excessive hormone production.'

'Twins? I can't believe it. Identical twins?'

'Fraternal twins.'

'I'm a fraternal twin,' she said. 'I have a twin brother.'

'Fraternal twins can be more likely to give

birth to twins,' the consultant said. 'You can have two girls, two boys, or one of each. But they're genetically different.'

Sally smiled. 'My brother and I are very close. I love being a twin.'

There were twins in Edward's family too.

The doctor talked to her some more about how to manage the nausea and how important it was for her not to become dehydrated and malnourished. She also explained how her antenatal care would differ from if she was having a 'singleton', including more visits to her GP and consultant. She asked about what role Sally's partner would play in her care, but didn't question her further when Sally stated flatly that she didn't have a partner. How different the experience would be if Edward was by her side; he'd proved himself to be so caring. She'd give anything for a bowl of his white rice so lovingly prepared.

After the consultant left, Sally lay back in the bed. *Twins*. She was delighted, if a little daunted. But in their father's country twins were considered bad luck. Another black mark against her suitability to be anything other than a secret in his life.

* * *

Later that afternoon the drip had done its job and Sally was feeling much better. She was able to eat a light meal and keep it down. The doctor wanted her to stay in hospital overnight for observation. She was okay with that. There was no one at home to keep an eye on her. Although, surprisingly, she suspected Hugo would if she asked him.

She had dressed back in her clothes and was sitting in the armchair in her room reading a magazine—she didn't feel like checking in to work and having to answer awkward questions—when a nurse popped her head around the door and asked if she felt up to having a visitor. 'Of course,' she said.

Hugo again, she was sure. Her brother was the only person who knew she was in hospital. It was sweet of him to come see her again. Maybe one day they could develop a better relationship.

She thought she was hallucinating when Edward walked into the room. She rubbed her eyes, but he was still there when she opened them. Edward, in a dark business suit and a cashmere coat, with a worried expression on his handsome face.

A great bolt of joy shot through her. 'Edward!'

She went to get up from her chair, but he was at her side in a second. 'No. Don't get up. Are you okay? I'm worried sick—'

She got up anyway. 'What are you doing here? How—?'

'I went to the Harrington Park Hotel, looking for you. I'd already been to your office. I met your brother Hugo. He was hostile. Gave me the third degree.'

Sally groaned. She could just imagine the reception Hugo had given him. Her brother could be quite formidable. 'I'm sorry about that.'

'Don't be. I would react in the same way for my sister in similar circumstances. He demanded to know if my intentions were honourable—'

She groaned again. 'Oh, no. How embarrassing.'

'He behaved as a good brother should. When I reassured him my intentions were indeed honourable, he told me where you were. Hospital. I got here as quickly as I could. Are you all right? I couldn't bear it if you weren't all right.'

He swept her into his arms and held her tight. *Back in Edward's arms.*

She breathed in the familiar scent of him and almost wept with happiness. 'I'm okay,' she said.

'And the baby?'

'Okay too.'

'Thank heaven. What happened? Hugo told me you fainted.'

'I was dehydrated, apparently. And anaemic. You know how sick and fatigued I was? It's an extreme form of morning sickness. All to do with an excess of a particular pregnancy hormone.'

'But why—?'

She took a deep breath and braced herself for his reaction. 'Because I'm pregnant with twins. That's why I started to show so early.'

'*Twins!* You're having twins?'

'Yes. And I refuse to believe they're bad luck or omens of ill tidings or whatever you believe in your country.'

'I don't believe that for one moment. And I think the old superstitions were probably only revived because of my uncles. They really were bad luck for the country. But not because they were twins.'

'You don't mind?'

'Why would I mind? As long as you're not at

any risk, I'm thrilled. Surely two babies are even better than one.'

'It doesn't make our situation any easier,' she said, feeling as though she should bring him back to reality.

'There is that,' he said. She wondered at the big grin on his face.

She frowned. 'Just what exactly are you doing in London? And seeking me out when we'd agreed we had no future?'

'I was utterly miserable after you left. I couldn't bear to be in the beach house without you. I went back to my apartment in the palace.'

'I... I've been miserable too,' she said in a classic understatement.

'I also got progressively angrier that my life was being determined for the sake of a political relationship with a neighbour who'd played the royal family for the last twenty years. I was furious my happiness was being sacrificed for no real gain. I demanded a meeting with my parents.'

'No petition required?'

'No.' Edward made a rather rude suggestion at what the petition could do to itself. 'I told them I refused to marry Princess Mai under any circumstances. That I would rather give up my right to the throne than spend my life with a woman I didn't love or indeed like. I might have mentioned she was an airhead.'

Sally gasped. 'How did they take it?'

'I didn't give them a chance to respond. It wasn't an empty threat. I have a private fortune; I could live very well not being Crown Prince. Then I told them all about you. My life has always been governed by honour and duty. I asked them what was the most honourable thing to do—to marry someone I didn't love and doom us both to a life of misery or to marry the mother of my child, a child who bears the blood of our ancestors.'

Even through her shock Sally noticed he didn't say he wanted to marry a woman he loved, rather the mother of his child. It made her feel somehow…diminished.

She realised she'd been holding her breath and let it out in a whoosh. 'What did they say?'

'They were too stunned to speak for a while. Then my father asked me more about you.'

'Like I had to pass an interview?'

'It wasn't like that. I told him how wonderful you are, how smart and clever and what a good family you came from.'

'Did you mention I've got an earl on my father's side and a duke on my mother's?'

'No. How could I? I had no idea.'

'It might have helped.'

'What helped, I think, was I told them how much I love you.'

She stood stock-still. 'You...you what?'

He looked down at her. 'I love you, Sally. I love you more than I could ever have imagined loving someone. I'm sorry I told them before I told you.' He paused. 'Do you think you could love me?'

Her breath caught on a sob. 'I already love you, Edward.'

'Really?' He smiled his wonderful smile. 'I knew I could love you that first day. My lovely mermaid.'

Her own smile felt wobbly around the edges. 'I didn't know how it felt to fall in love. So I didn't recognise it when it happened. Looking back, I realise I fell for you then too. But it was during our time in the bachelor house. That's when I really knew what it meant to love.'

He kissed her, a long tender kiss full of promise and love and sheer bubbling happiness. Her heart, that had shattered into so many pieces, felt whole again now Edward had a hold on it and bloomed with joy.

'So what happened with your parents?' Sally asked eventually.

'They gave me permission to marry you.'

'They did? They seriously released you from the engagement? To marry me?'

'Now you've got royal approval, I'm hoping you won't disappoint the King and Queen. More importantly, that you won't disappoint me. Will you marry me, Sally?'

She thought about how much she valued her independence. But how miserable she'd been without him. And how much she wanted to share her pregnancy and the birth of their children with him. Most of all, how deeply she loved him.

'Yes. I want to share my life with you. I'll gladly marry you, Edward.'

They shared another long, sweet kiss.

'What made your parents change their minds?'

'My original petition had made them think, they said. They married for love and have a very happy marriage. My mother said they didn't want to deny their son the same chance of happiness. I suspect she guessed there might be someone special who I wasn't mentioning.'

'So you're officially released from your agreement with Princess Mai?'

'I hadn't actually got engaged. But yes.'

'That's just wonderful. I—'

He put up his hand. 'Wait. There's more.'

'More conditions, more—?'

'After I thanked them and they'd thanked me for all my service to the Crown and how they wouldn't dream of letting me step down from my royal role and of course I must do the honourable thing by you, they told me that Princess Mai had refused to marry me.'

'What?' Sally laughed. *'No.'*

'Yes. Apparently, she said I was too old for her and she refused to be forced into marriage.'

'Thank you, Mai. I wonder if she's met someone else.'

'Good luck to her if she has. My parents are pleased because they have gained significant bargaining power. They reluctantly agreed to say that the arrangement was broken by mutual consent and not by the Princess defying her father, so as to save face for Mai's father, the King.'

'That must surely mean he becomes indebted to your parents.'

'And my parents will save face when I soon marry such a smart, beautiful woman as you.'

'So we're political pawns anyway. Whichever way we look at it.'

'That's the way it is and it's unlikely to change. Do you mind?'

'I'll have to learn to get used to it. But no, I don't mind. All I want is for us to be together, and to bring up our children together.'

'We won't have to live in my country the whole time. I need to spend time in Singapore. And we have a magnificent apartment in Mayfair.'

'And the bachelor house. I love it there.'

'Of course, the bachelor house. Can we marry as soon as possible?' he said.

'Yes, please. I can't wait to be your wife.' She laughed. 'Besides, we'll need to walk down the aisle before I start to show too much. These twins are growing by the second.'

'Actually, in our culture it's not such a terrible thing for a bride to be visibly pregnant on her wedding day. It proves she's fertile.'

'I've got a lot to learn about your culture and what's expected of me as a Tianlipinese,' she said.

'And as Crown Princess.'

She gasped. 'I'll be a *princess*. I… I hadn't thought any further than being Mrs Edward Chen.'

'You'll be her too. As well as Sally, Crown Princess of Tianlipin.'

'Wow! That's a lot to assimilate. I need a crash course in being a royal. And I'll have to start learning the language immediately. I want to be the best wife I can. And best princess too, I guess. Not to mention mother.'

'I'll be only too happy to help guide you. My family will love you. Jennifer already does. But no one could love you as much as I do.'

They kissed again, a long sweet kiss.

'May I ask one thing of you?' she said.

'Anything,' he said.

'Can we be here in London together for our Christmas Eve launch party at the Harrington Park? It's a big deal for me and my brothers.'

'Of course. I know how much it means to you.'

'I want you to be by my side when I hang my ornament on the tree for the first time since I was a little girl.'

'I will always be by your side,' he said. 'As the husband who adores you.'

EPILOGUE

London, Christmas Eve, one year later

SALLY STOOD VERY close to Edward, looking up at the splendidly decorated Harrington Park Hotel Christmas tree. It was the same tree, just a little taller, that had starred in the winter wonderland she'd designed for the previous year. The relaunch party had been such a success the garden had been replicated for this year—and would be every Christmas, her brother Hugo had declared.

Last year she and Edward had stood in front of the tree, newly engaged, ecstatic to be together but not quite certain what the new year would bring. She had placed her white Merlion ornament—which had been much admired—on the tree on behalf of her unborn twins and wondered what her new life would bring.

This year Sally—now Crown Princess Sally of Tianlipin—held their baby son Harry in her arms, while Edward held their daughter Kate, named after Sally's mother. The adorable black-haired twins were only five months old, so they needed a little help in hanging their ornaments on the tree. Just like baby Sally had needed help from her father.

The exquisite hand-blown glass ornaments had been especially produced in Tianlipin to Sally's design. They were inspired by traditional silk lanterns and finished with red silk tassels. There was a yellow one for Kate and a red one for Harry—both auspicious colours. She wanted to bring a touch of Tianlipin, where she was so happy, into the rejuvenated Harrington Park, her childhood home.

As the twins lifted their little arms up to the tree—their parents with a firm grip on both babies and ornaments—there were oohs and aahs from an audience of party-goers that included Hugo and Jay, hotel guests and the staff—including some of the original staff who had known Sally as a child.

'Happy?' Edward asked. Her beloved husband Edward, who she loved more each day they were together. They often mused together how very fortunate it was that she had fallen into that pool.

'Very happy,' she said. 'It's good to be back in London for Christmas.'

'We can come back here every Christmas for you to spend it with your brothers at the hotel,' he said.

'I'd like that very much.'

She realised she'd allowed her odious stepfather to kill Christmas for her but now, celebrating the season with her beloved husband, children and brothers brought her a renewed sense of joy and wonder. There was gratitude too, for her new life. The Christmas spirit filled her heart.

She'd had some trepidation about marrying into the royal family but, as Edward had predicted, they had welcomed her. She wasn't the first English spouse in their history, her father-in-law the King had commented. He'd praised her for her efforts to learn the language and study the culture and history of her adopted country. Her mother-in-law had been reserved at first but had come into her own when the twins were born, supporting and helping Sally as much as she could. The Queen was a doting grandmother and helped ease some of Sally's sadness that her own mother wasn't there to see her grandbabies. Jennifer had become a true friend; Sally could envisage working with her when the twins got older. She'd sold her company to her business partners when she'd got married.

The twins' ornaments successfully attached to the tree, Edward swept her into a loving hug that encompassed his wife and both their children, who squealed their delight. 'Happy Christmas, my darling mermaid,' he said. 'I'm glad you're happy to be home.'

'If you mean home is wherever you and our babies are, yes, I couldn't be happier,' she said, kissing him.

* * * * *

LET'S TALK
Romance

For exclusive extracts, competitions and special offers, find us online:

f facebook.com/millsandboon

⊙ @millsandboonuk

🐦 @millsandboon

Or get in touch on 0844 844 1351*

For all the latest titles coming soon, visit millsandboon.co.uk/nextmonth

Want even more
ROMANCE?

Join our bookclub today!

Visit millsandbook.co.uk/Bookclub and save on brand new books.

MILLS & BOON